Melanie Hughes was brougl   ... trained
at the Central School of Speech and Drama. She went on
to act in theatre, television and films. She began writing
for Ken Russell in the television series "Lady Chatterley"
and then worked on further projects for him, the BBC,
London Films, and Union Pictures. Her first published
book was *Mrs Fisher's Tulip*.
Melanie loves art, theatre, films, reading and the sea.

War Changes Everything

"I couldn't put this fantastic story down; it's wonderful,
so involving and naturally and effortlessly written, it was a
real delight."

Paul Anthony Barber

War Changes Everything

War Changes Everything

Melanie Hughes

Patrician Press
Manningtree

First published as a paperback edition by Patrician Press 2017

E-book edition published by Patrician Press 2017

British Library Cataloguing in Publication Data. A catalogue record for this book is available from the British Library.

ISBN paperback edition 978-0-9955386-5-8

ISBN e-book edition 978-0-9955386-4-1

www.patricianpress.com

Published by Patrician Press 2017

For more information: www.patricianpress.com

For Mike and Ilona with love

In Memoriam
Juanita Serracante Bruce 1916-2005
Kanwar Lal Amol Singh 1920-1982

This is the true story of a woman whose life was defined by war. Like many of her generation, the freedoms that we take for granted were forged fitfully and painfully by their lives. There were no guidelines for them. They were modern women in a not yet modern age. The flotsam and jetsam of war.

Chapter One

I am nearly a hundred years old and I still can't make sense of any of it, though I have spent most of my life trying. Now that I am very old and my time on earth is short, my days are long, the hours pass slowly and I spend most of them thinking about the past and wondering why.

I learnt early on that life is bleak with few moments of joy. That there are things you do that you can never come back from. No matter how sad and sorry you are.

My mother was a Bruce. She was born on the Isle of Skye. When she was two, her family moved to England where my grandmother was known as 'the best looking woman in South Shields.' Apparently, she was tall and dark like me. I wouldn't know. I never met her.

Mother came to London when she was seventeen. The First World War had just started. She got a job as a chambermaid in a hotel in the West End. That was where she met my father, a man I never knew. Jaime Serracante.

He was Spanish, a Catalan, and she loved him very much. I know almost nothing about him other than his name. It was the old story—a whirlwind love affair—he woos, loves and leaves her. She never hears from him again, but soon discovers she is pregnant. Her desperate letters are returned unanswered. He gave her nothing—not even his name.

I was born a bastard. Her family disowned her. None of them wanted to have anything to do with either of us. Except her brother, Duncan. He came to see her in London on his way to the front. Apparently, he hugged her, held me in his arms and told her not to worry. On his next leave we would all go home together. He said, "When Ma sees the bairn, she'll change her tune. Bonnie little lass, isn't she? You'll be all right, Sis," he promised, "No-one will hurt you while I'm around."

He was killed on the first day of the Battle of the Somme. He was nineteen and I was one. He was the only member of my family I ever laid eyes on and I can't remember him at all.

After that we were alone. My eighteen-year-old mother and her bastard child. No friends or family, no means of support.

Fortunately for us both, my mother was tough. She had that Scots stoicism that can withstand disaster. The granite in the soul. She never analysed and she never indulged in self-pity. Either was an anathema to her. She had made her bed and she would lie in it. Come what may.

She never cried and would not permit me to. We had to get on with it. Our survival depended on it and she never let either of us forget it.

The hotel sacked her when she began to be sick in the mornings. "No pregnant chamber maids in this establishment, thank you very much!" they said and out she went with a dispatch that left her reeling. But Mother refused to become one of life's casualties. She could be knocked down, but she was damned if she would stay there.

She found herself another job. A definite step down. Scrubbing and cleaning. Maid-of-all-work, I think, they called it. A skivvy really: no wages, just her keep. She took it because no-one else would take her and to "keep a roof over our heads," she later told me. Already when I was just a fluttering shadow inside her, she talked in terms of "us". I always thought that was a measure of the woman she was.

She worked hard and got lucky. Mrs Lomasney was an eccentric old lady, living alone in Kensington, clinging to the fringes of gentility. She'd had a "past" apparently and she grew fond of the little Scots girl who cried herself to sleep at night, but worked like a Trojan all day long.

Early one autumn morning, my mother crept into Mrs Lomasney's bedroom, as she did every morning, to light the fire. She told me she always tried to be quiet as a mouse so as not to wake her mistress. But Mrs Lomasney was awake—in every sense. She asked Mother outright when the baby was due. Mother told me she began to shake and dropped a piece of coal on the carpet, certain she was about to be 'shown the door'.

"January," she mumbled miserably.

Mrs Lomasney nodded and said nothing. Mother picked up the coal and scuttled out. She waited all day for the axe to fall. It didn't. Instead the Cook/Housekeeper grudgingly told her she was to be put on 'light duties'. No more heavy coal scuttles or scrubbing area steps for her. Just polishing brass and silver, light dusting, a bit of mending. On Mrs Lomasney's orders. When my mother tried to thank her employer, she just replied, "Oh I know where you are. And I know the place to be a hard one."

She was Irish and had a heart of gold, but she didn't like to be caught at it. She had a horror of being taken advantage of. She'd had a hard life, Mother said, but she would never tell me why. "Not my secret to tell," she would say when asked. And that was it. You could have put her on the rack and it would have made no difference. They never told in those days. They believed in secrets and lies.

I was born on the 6th January. Epiphany—the feast of the Magi. There were no Wise Men in attendance at my birth. Mrs Lomasney delivered me on the kitchen table of the house in Peel Street. My mother was too ashamed to go to the hospital. It was a difficult birth—I came out feet first—a botched and bloody beginning that nearly killed us both. Mrs Lomasney had to send for the doctor in the end. He huffed and puffed, muttering that Mother should have gone to the hospital. But he knew very well why she had not. Anyway, he gave the orders; Mrs Lomasney pulled me out and he stitched up Mother. He pronounced me "hale and hearty." Then he demanded his fee. That was Mrs Lomasney's cue to huff and puff. She said she didn't see why he would charge a full fee when she had "done all the spadework for him." She got very Irish about it, my mother said. They had a big row.

Mrs Lomasney would always get very Irish in moments of high emotion. She and my mother were very similar in that respect. When they got worked up—anger, joy or despair—their thin veneer of Englishness would vanish and they would both revert to type with a vengeance. "The old countries" came storming through. They were alarmingly alike. They laughed at the same jokes, cried at the same sentimental songs, and loved the same food. My mother was what she called "a good plain cook"—her specialities were the stew she called Scottish and Mrs Lomasney insisted was Irish, sponge cakes and Cullen Skink. She also baked very good bread. She didn't believe in the shop bought kind. She announced "the English can't bake bread to save their lives," then she rolled up her sleeves and made her own.

The Cook/Housekeeper, whose food was awful apparently, lumpy sauces and stews of "nothing but the finest gristle," took umbrage and stormed out, muttering about Scottish cows and bastard brats. Mrs Lomasney didn't turn a hair, she yelled "Good riddance" and slammed the door behind her. Then turning to my mother she said, "Stuck up bitch. Never did like her. Do you think you can fill her shoes?"

Mother did. And she pointed out that she would do so without selling off all the surplus food ordered by Cook, who had sold it on at a profit. A little side line that had been her only culinary speciality.

And so we lived quite contentedly until the end of the war. When my mother was busy with the chores, Mrs Lomasney would tend to me, sitting for hours in her big chair by the fire with me in her arms. We were happy—then the war ended and Cornelius came home. He was Mrs Lomasney's son. He was a good looking man, dapper and well-dressed. He also had a good job. He was a senior clerk in the HMSO in Whitehall. But if he hadn't been mad before the war, he certainly was after it. Whether it was because he had had a bad time in the trenches—he would never speak of it, but regularly woke screaming and shaking, drenched in sweat, drowning in his nightmares—or because he had been gassed which had permanently damaged his lungs and possibly also his brain, I don't know, but he was truly insane. Nowadays he would be in a locked ward. But then they just chucked them out of the army and sent them home. To sink or swim as the case might be and take their unfortunate families with them.

Cornelius would change in an instant from a quiet, withdrawn man to a screaming devil, who thought nothing of punching and kicking his elderly mother for no apparent reason. He should have been treated. But psychiatry was in its infancy then, and Mrs Lomasney, like many of her generation, had a horror of it. She would no more have put her son in an asylum than she would have poisoned his stew. In her eyes it was much the same thing. And she may have been right, but her blind adoration of him meant that we were all defenceless in the face of his violence.

After he had attacked her, she would pick herself up, ask Mother to fetch a brandy for her nerves and a steak for her black eye, and tend to the sobbing, remorseful wretch that was her son. He was always inconsolable after he had beaten her. He knew exactly what he had done, he just didn't know why. He couldn't help it, he said. It came upon him out of nowhere, without any apparent cause or provocation. Afterwards, he would lie on the floor in a foetal position, crunched in despair and when he was like that only my mother could reach him. She would talk quietly to him and, although he could not reply, his eyes would latch on to her and never leave her face. She was like the beacon of a lighthouse to him. Her blunt kindness was the only thing that got through to him and he came to worship her. At that time she never bore the brunt of his rage. Then he would follow her round like a little dog and sit for hours in the kitchen, while she cooked and cleaned and soon he found he could not do without her.

Mrs Lomasney decided they should marry. Mother did

not want to, but she wasn't in much of a position to argue. She hoped, at first she said, that she could calm him down and that he would be a father to me.

Chapter Two

Cornelius hated me. I never knew why or what I had done to provoke his loathing. Perhaps I did nothing, perhaps my mere being was enough. I was too physical a reminder that my mother had enjoyed a fruitful coupling with another man. Perhaps looking at my face he didn't see me at all, but Jaime Serracante, whose absent but dominant shadow lay across us all, turning me into a social outcast and him into second best.

Cornelius made my childhood a misery. When he was calm, he ignored me. He always spoke to my mother as if they were alone in the room. Any childish prattle or questions asked were never answered. I learned never to address him. From a very early age, I ate my evening meal alone in the kitchen. I was banished as far as possible to the periphery of their lives.

When he was angry, I was beaten, learning the sting and shame of a split lip and a blackened eye long before I could read or write. His rage seemed boundless, my tears could not move him. He terrified me. I dreaded his return from work in the evenings, running away to hide in bed and silence long before I had any need of sleep. His shadow in the hall, falling across my bedroom door, was enough to make my throat constrict with terror and my stomach knot with fear.

Mother tried to compensate. His behaviour hurt her as she watched him hurting me. She would interpose herself between us, taking the blows that were meant for me. But it was useless. He would punch her face and stomach and then throw her aside like an unwanted doll. Once he beat her so badly we had to get the doctor. He knocked her out and when she did not get up, I crouched beside her, taking her hand and stroking her face, begging her to come back. To no avail. She remained unconscious. He glared at me as I started to cry, then gave her recumbent form a parting kick and turning as he walked through the door said, "She's just play acting." I think it was the only remark he ever addressed to me directly. Then he went out. I ran to get Mrs Lomasney, who dried my tears and sent for the doctor. My mother was in hospital for a week. Mrs Lomasney and I went to see her every day. He never went once. While she was there and as a result of his beating, she lost the child she had been carrying. The one neither he nor I knew anything about. When Mrs Lomasney told him about it, he wept, great gulping sobs that shook his shoulders and ran down his crumpled face.

"You see, Cornelius," she said sternly, "by your wickedness, you have lost the thing you most wanted. It is God's punishment." He wept harder when she said that. But I was glad. I didn't want any more children. Certainly not his. I was pleased he had been punished. It was nothing he did not deserve.

Mother could not have any more children after that. Mrs Lomasney told me the day before Mother came home. She told me to be especially kind to Mother because of "her loss". But as I have said, I was glad of it. And gladder still because it seemed to bring us closer together. Mother and I were now an exclusive alliance that could never be shared with another. Bonded by our fear and hatred of him. You could see it in her face when we heard his key in the lock at night. He took to spending more and more time out. When he returned from the pub, falling down drunk, she would put him to bed and then she would creep quietly into mine, while I pretended to be asleep. Both of us as far away from him as we could get under the same roof.

And so we went on—poles apart, but chained together like convicts until one day the fragile link that bound us together broke.

Mrs Lomasney became ill. She had gradually been growing frailer, but because we all loved her, we all pitched in to shore her up. She was the only point of reference in our lives; an oasis of sanity in the one man lunatic asylum that was our home. Her frailty brought out the best in us.

We became kinder, even to each other, but most of all to her. The woman whose love for each of us had been our salvation.

We hoped we could shield her from her own mortality. Then one day, as she was sitting in the kitchen, watching my mother kneading bread while I washed up, she dropped her cup of tea. I watched the delicate pink and gilt cup smash and the warm liquid pool on the cold flagstones. I loved those cups, with their thin gilt handles and fluted edges. Mrs Lomasney looked up at my mother with fear in her eyes.

"I can't feel my right hand, Beth. I have no feeling in it. None at all." She was horrified and tearful. I felt as if the sky had fallen in. Mother bustled to reassure her and clear up the mess, sending me for the doctor. He came at once. He examined Mrs Lomasney for a long time and then came downstairs to talk to my mother. He looked grim.

My mother spoke first, her voice dry and hesitant as if her throat hurt.

"Is she...?" She couldn't even get the words out.

He nodded, then said softly, "Yes. She needs to be in hospital now."

My mother's eyes filled with tears. "She hates hospitals. Could we not look after her at home?"

"Only if you're certain you can cope. Otherwise it won't be a kindness."

"We're not handing her over to strangers." The granite was back.

The doctor nodded again, "All right. If you're sure. It won't be long. I'll come back in a few days to see how you're coping." With that, he left us. But Mother's word was her law. Once given, there was no going back.

"You'll have to tell *him*," I said before the door had closed behind the doctor.

"Aye. I will. And for once he'll have to put someone else first. I'll make sure of that."

She did too. When Cornelius returned from work she brought him into the kitchen and shut the door. I could hear from the soft Scots lilt in her voice how upset she was. Then a harsh discordant cry—the cry of an animal in pain. And my mother very firmly, "That's enough. There'll be plenty of time to cry when she can't hear you. Now she comes first."

We put everything else aside. The norms of our lives fell away, unwanted, unnecessary. No regular school for me, no evenings in the pub for him, no chatting with the neighbours on the area steps for her.

We became a team. Mother nursed and cooked the delicate broths that were all Mrs Lomasney could eat, and together she and I cleaned, washed and bathed our patient. When we were not working, we sat with her and sang to her. She liked that. She would smile her now lopsided smile and beat time on the sheet with her one good hand and we would launch into her old favourites, 'Molly Malone' and 'Danny Boy'. Those were the ones she loved best. And we sang as if our lives depended on it.

Cornelius spent every minute he could with her. Holding her hand, gently trying to allay her fear. A strange reversal of roles. Because she was afraid as one by one she lost the threads of herself. She lost her speech, her smile, and then her sight. In the end I was banished from her room because her roaming sightless eyes and desperate, meaningless shouts frightened me. I was put on kitchen duty—scrubbing, washing, peeling. I worked all the time and I was happy to. Apart from my mother, Mrs Lomasney was the only human soul who had ever loved me and I loved her back. I prayed for her to get well, promising God everything I could think of if He would only make her better. I even stole a penny from the kitchen jar—an act I knew would bring a terrible retribution, but I didn't care. I took it straight to Mrs Lomasney's church and lit a candle for her. I had seen her do that often. I knew if you did that God would know it was a special prayer and it would be heeded. She had told me so.

When I came home I owned up and waited for my punishment. My mother was sad but resigned and would have punished me, but Cornelius looked hard at me, still the same cold dislike in his eyes, then he said, "Leave it. Let it go." Then he went upstairs to join the empty shell that had been his mother. It was never mentioned again.

In the end, they both slept in the room with her. He on a little couch at the foot of the bed and she in the big chair beside it. Always at hand, always nearby, talking softly, holding her hand. We were all with her when she died.

My mother woke me in the middle of the night. "She's going now. Come and say goodbye." So I went and kissed the still warm cheek and tried not to be frightened by the rasping breath. Cornelius stood silently by her, holding her hand. I have never seen anyone in so much pain. He was utterly still, barely breathing, frozen with grief. In spite of everything, at that moment I felt sorry for him. I still do.

The rasping breaths merged into each other and grew quieter. Then she gave a soft sigh and opened her eyes wide as if in astonishment; their soft brown velvet dark and burning in her pale and wasted face. We watched as the light went out of them and she was gone, taking all her secrets and her great kindness with her. Mother reached across and closed her eyes, tears running from her own.

Cornelius stood as if made of stone. He could neither move nor speak. I went back to my room, leaving them alone with her. During the night I heard him cry—the tearing sobs of an abandoned child and my mother must have stayed with him, because she did not come to me that night.

He walked through the following days like a ghost. He neither ate nor slept nor spoke—not even when the priest came to see him. The day of the funeral came and when the hearse arrived with its flower decked coffin and plumed black horses. The neighbours came out to pay their respects. My mother and I, in deepest black, took our places behind the hearse and waited, but Cornelius was nowhere to be found. We waited for some time, but in the end my mother nodded at the undertaker and said in her softest Scots, "Well, it cannot hurt her now." So Mrs Lomasney was buried with no kith or kin to mourn her, only the lost girl and the child that she had saved.

Cornelius returned late that night. Long after the last sherry had been drunk and the leftover cakes and sandwiches cleared away. He was drunk. We heard the fumbling of the key in the lock and then the heavy stumbling and falling on the stairs. My mother blew out our candle and took me in her arms. We were one again, welded together by fear.

The next few days taught us what we could expect. Crazy with loss, he punished us. We were beaten without mercy. We hid in the house, bruised and battered, like animals gone to earth, while he attempted to assuage his grief with rage. If he was mad before, he was doubly so afterwards. He had lost the only thread that had tethered him to sanity.

The beatings went on. I have often wondered if he would have killed one of us, but before he could the outside world intervened. My teacher at school asked me why I had an almost permanent black eye. I dared not reply, so she wrote and asked Mother to come in and see her. I have no idea what was said, but Mother emerged from this meeting flushed with shame. We didn't speak on the bus on the way home, but I knew she wasn't cross with me because she bought me a gingerbread man from the bakery on the corner. She never bought baked goods. She did not mention it again.

The following morning when Cornelius came down as usual for his breakfast she shooed me out into the basement area to play. It was no use. I could hear every word. She told him firmly that she had been called into school to explain why I was always covered in bruises and that if it were to continue, we would leave.

"You can't," he said smugly, barely looking up, pouring tea into his saucer to drink. "You gave your oath to a dying woman." He looked up then. "You promised her you'd look after me."

"I did. But I didn't promise her I'd let you murder my child and I promise you, Cornelius, if you lay a finger on that child again I will walk out of that door and you will never see either of us again."

Just where she thought we were going to go I have no idea. I was frightened. Home was hell, but it was the only home I had ever known and I was scared of leaving it. But she spoke as if she meant it and he believed her. She was now his only guy-rope. Without her, he may well have been institutionalised. Anyway, after that he barely spoke to either of us. My mother became more his housekeeper than his wife, which suited us. What was more important the beatings stopped and for that we were profoundly grateful.

For two years we carried on like the survivors of a shipwreck, cut off from the world and each other, stumbling on, unable to get our bearings. Then something happened to change the humdrum numbness of our lives, or mine at least. I won a scholarship. It turned out I was clever.

Chapter Three

No one was more surprised than me. I was a shy, unadventurous child, prone to daydreams and silence. It was always best to say nothing. There was so much to hide. Ordinary day-to-day life in London then was rigid and rule bound. It ran unswervingly on train tracks of convention. Not for the gilded few, perhaps, but for the dun brown rest of us it was constrained and bigoted.

I had sidled through primary school an unremarked shadow, never reproved—I didn't dare be naughty—never encouraged. Until I sat the Eleven-plus. I sailed through that with flying colours. All those imprisoned evenings, hiding in my room, nose in a book, desperate for escape even by proxy, had paid off. I was awarded a scholarship to the Godolphin and Latymer School for Girls, one of the most prestigious day schools in London. They offered to educate me for nothing until matriculation, and they would provide all books, uniform, lunches and sports gear.

They wrote to my mother to tell her so. The day the letter arrived, she kept it in her apron pocket all day long, taking it out and reading it over and over. Smiling and showing it to neighbours, friends, the milkman—anyone who came into her orbit. Even Cornelius. When he returned from work that evening, she was still foolish with pride. She held the letter out for him to read. He didn't bother, just raked us both with a glance of pure contempt and said,

"Her? They're pulling your leg."

"They are not." She was still smiling. He snatched the letter from her hand and read it, scowling as he read the bit about my having scored more than eighty-five percent in all subjects.

"Must be a mistake. Look at her. She can barely string two words together. They're having a laugh."

He threw the letter on the kitchen table and walked out. We waited to hear the front door slam. Then hugged each other in silent joy. We didn't dare laugh or cry— in case he heard and came back.

But a few weeks later a new hell emerged. I had to be registered. A procedure that required proof of identity. In those days that could only mean a birth certificate. Mine—on which it was blindingly obvious that my parents' surnames were not the same and that mine was the same as my mother's.

The woman in the school office took the document. Then she read it and looked at us both with the particular cold stare that would become very familiar. Until I married that was the response that greeted every occasion when proof of my identity was required. She said pointedly, "Oh." A whole world of prejudice was contained in that short syllable. In future, she would always look at me as if I were something dirty, contaminating.

She got up and went into the Head Mistress' office. They both came out. Identical in their lace-up shoes and thick lisle stockings. I thought that was it. I was going to be cast out for the vermin I was. They looked at us in silence for a moment, taking us in with their smooth grey hair and cold grey eyes. Then the Head Mistress shook her head and said, "I don't think there's anything we can do, Miss Beaumont. Sadly. The results speak for themselves." Then looking reproachfully at Mother and me, as if we had pulled off an elaborate con trick, she went back into her study and shut the door. Leaving Miss Beaumont to do the dirty work. Which she did with unconcealed bad grace. My date and place of birth, school history and address were all noted. Then as she entered my name in the school register, she pulled a face and said, "How on earth do you pronounce that?" Her disbelief and distaste almost tangible. I didn't blame her. I hated it myself. Juanita Serracante Bruce. A name less likely to allow me to fade into the background could hardly have been imagined. What had Mother been thinking of? My wretched father and her vain hopes for his return. In branding me as his, she sought to bring him back to her. I cursed her for it. All my life it was the cause of astonishment and even mirth.

"Blimey, love," the dinner lady said as she asked my name on the first day, while dolloping a huge mound of cottage pie onto my plate, "How'dya come by a name like that? Sounds more like a music hall turn." Indeed. The girls around me laughed and I was bathed in humiliation and shame. I took my plate and sat down at an empty table in the corner of the vast dining hall, as far from the others as I could get. I put my head down so no-one could see the tears and forked the congealing grey mush around my plate. I knew I would have to eat it. I just couldn't see how.

A plate was banged down on the table. "Budge up." It was an order so I obeyed it.

"Take no notice. They're idiots." She sat down beside me. I dared a peep. She was an older girl aged about fourteen, with glossy raven hair and satiny olive skin. She tried a mouthful of pie.

"Putrid, isn't it? Pig swill, I call it." I think I dared to laugh. She pushed her plate away. Then went on briskly, "Your name's Juanita?" She pronounced it oddly as if it was spelled with a Y not the hard J of our pronunciation. I nodded, still ashamed.

"Well," she said taking a gulp of water, "S' the only name in this place that's as daft as mine." She held out her hand. "Yolanda Barroni." You could see her point. "I'm Italian. You must be Spanish."

We shook hands. "We'd better stick together, Latins and all. *Contra mundem.* Talk about eyeless in Gaza." She paused, as if considering our fate. Then went on, "You've got to pity them really, this lot," taking in the whole room with a scornful glance, "they're all called things like Frances Higginbottom or Deidre Dripnose. Ugly as sin, in name and deed."

Then she put her elbows on the table and began to talk. She had a low, gravelly voice and a surprisingly gruff laugh.

I had always thought I was ugly. I didn't look like other children. Everything about me was wrong. My hair was too dark, my skin too pale and I was tall and skinny. Cornelius always said I looked like a stick insect. But this girl, this Yolanda, was talking to me as if I was like her. Different, but in a good way, almost special.

Yolanda may have been only fourteen, but she had style. And a kind of robust courage, a willingness to swim against the tide I came to admire and love. We did stick together. Despite the difference in our ages and backgrounds, we became best friends.

My school days quickly took on the same pattern as before. Reading, learning, keeping my head down. But the scope of my studies was different and I discovered the heady, insecure joy of learning. As a new avenue of thought opened up before me, I felt the same excitement others feel at the prospect of a long journey. I began to haunt the Kensington Library in the holidays and on the long Saturday afternoons. For me, it became a treasure trove and a refuge. I read everything I could lay my hands on, hoping to find a means of understanding and escape.

My world, although still grey, was opening out. But

what truly flooded my horizon with light was Yolanda. She brought colour and verve into my life, and a bright breezy insouciance that was as foreign as it was welcome. She lived in a tall, narrow house in Mornington Crescent where chaos reigned, with a shouting, laughing family and a huge cast of rotating cousins. Her family owned a business in Soho, importing pasta, olive oil and salamis to West End hotels and restaurants. It was all very unusual then. What is commonplace now on our supermarket shelves was then a peculiar rarity, and the exotic was generally viewed with extreme suspicion. Foreign was almost a term of abuse.

Yolanda and I met often. We spent most of our free time together. She would winkle me out of the library and we would spend whole days walking though London, in all seasons and weathers, making it our own. We both took it utterly for granted that we would end up by going to her home. We never went to mine. We window-shopped in Regent and Bond Street, peeped into the grand restaurants and hotels her father supplied, took refuge from the rain in the dusty, deserted museums, and walked until exhaustion took over, always ending up at the Barroni home.

I loved it. It was full of life and laughter. The sullen, terrified silences of my home had no place there. The Barronis had fun together. They yelled and fought often; sudden angry squalls that would erupt like a summer storm and die down just as quickly, then they made up and loved each other with a fierce possessive passion that astonished and enthralled me. Everything they did was loud and colourful. Bright silks were draped over their furniture and windows. Opera was played constantly on a scratchy, wind up gramophone, not with church-like reverence but with real love and familiarity. It was sung along to, sending great ballooning waves of sound throughout the whole house.

Books were read and handed round. Rarely put back in the bookcase but left out, at the ready, for the talks and rows that would ensue. The careless largesse of their lives made me feel giddy at first, almost drunk. And indeed it was in their house that I sipped my first glass of wine and tasted olives and garlic. Mama B (as everyone, even me eventually, called her) was very kind. The first time I met her, standing in the doorway, afraid to come in and frozen with shyness, she seemed to sum me up at a glance, reading the truth of my life far more accurately in my silence and averted gaze than anything I could or would have told her. She smiled at me and her smile flowed over me like balm.

Later Yolanda told me that after I had left she joined Mama in the kitchen. She sat down at the table and pulled the biscuit tin towards her.

"She's nice, isn't she?"

Mama was busy with her ragù and did not reply.

"I like her a lot."

"I thought so."

A moment of concern. Then, as ever with Yolanda, defiance.

"I like her because... she's interesting."

Still Mama did not reply.

"She had an awful time when she first came to school. They were laughing at her."

Then her coup de grace. "Because of her name."

Still no comment. Never one to give up, Yolanda went on.

"And she has a rotten time at home too. Her stepfather hates her."

Mama turned round at that and forgot to stir her ragù.

"The thing is her mother..."

I had told Yolanda the truth right from the start, knowing instinctively that she could handle anything but lies.

"Stop, Yolanda. Stop right there." Mama wiped her hands and moved to chop the herbs waiting on the draining board.

"I am a practising Catholic. Don't tell me anything that will force me to hurt her."

She brandished the mezza luna like a weapon. "But Mama..."

"No." She began chopping vigorously. "I don't want to hear it. What I don't know can't hurt her. I have the feeling she has already had too much of that."

She turned away and that was it. Discussion over. Yolanda told me all of this and then added at the end that sometimes her Mama drove her nuts. I think she expected me to agree or at least commiserate. But I knew that Mama Barroni knew exactly what I was and that she would never let that knowledge hurt me. She was a devout Catholic. Crucifixes, Madonnas and statues of Jesus were to be found in every nook and niche of her home, but prayer formed the foundation of her life, not the bars around it.

Yolanda didn't exactly have an easy ride at school either. Her air of assurance and her pride fooled me at first into thinking she took it all in her stride, but my eyes were opened one day in that first autumn term when we trudged round the playground in the drizzling rain. None of the other girls would include us in their games.

One particular girl, Susan Waldron, had taken a complete dislike to me and I couldn't for the life of me understand why. "I never did anything to her."

"You don't have to. They hate anyone different, let alone foreign." I was not consoled because I wasn't foreign, only my name was.

"One genius even told me Italians eat worms. She said she knew it for a fact cos she'd seen it in a restaurant."

She raked the playground and its occupants with a glance that would have done an empress proud.

"I presume she'd seen someone eating spaghetti and it shook her to the core." She looked down at our feet.

"They could really hurt you if they weren't such fools."

I said nothing because I knew they had hurt her. And also because I wasn't too sure what spaghetti was myself.

The meals at the Barronis floored me at first. Strange thick soups full of bright coloured vegetables, then a clear one with bits of raw egg stirred in that looked repulsive but tasted delicious; sweet smelling sauces made with garlic and herbs, velvety and smooth after bubbling away on the stove for ages. And then the spaghetti! That fazed me completely. I could not get the knack of winding it onto my fork. It just slithered and slid back onto my plate with a will of its own. After what seemed like hours, sweaty with effort, I was nearly in tears. Yolanda and her brothers laughed, then she hissed at me.

"Just leave it. You don't have to eat it." But I couldn't. It seemed so rude. So I kept on trying until Mama B rescued me. She sort of cut it up and gave me a spoon. I felt so ashamed. Like some sort of stupid baby.

After that she only served lovely little pasta shells when I was there. They were easy to eat and I loved them. But not as much as the ice cream. That was heaven. It was a real treat in those days because very few people had refrigerators. Their ice cream was soft and silky and made with real fruit. Peaches and cherries, strawberries and funny green nuts called pistachios. It was utter bliss.

Mamma B loved flowers. In all seasons she had flowers in bowls scattered around the house. Any flowers, she wasn't particular. But once, early on, I shyly presented her with a rather crushed bunch of violets I had bought for a farthing. I wanted to thank her for the many meals she had insisted I share with them. Food that at first attracted me, but also scared me a bit because it was so different, so alien.

Anyway, I presented her with these flowers and she hugged me with real delight. Exclaiming to everyone in the house how beautiful they were, remarking on their colour and scent. She said they were her favourites, that they had grown in the woods near her home in Italy and a rush of pleasure flowed over me.

Yolanda groaned. "We'll never hear the end of this. How did you know they were her favourites?"

"I didn't. I just hoped she'd like them."

"You've done it now. She'll love you forever. No escape."

I didn't want one. I wanted to pretend even for a few seconds that I was loved and approved of. It went straight to my head like their wine. I felt I was at last part of something. The Barronis took me to their hearts and they were the first real joy in mine.

I told Mother all about it. At first she was curious and asked a lot of questions, wanting to know everything. What they looked like, how old they were, what the house was like and, above all, what the food was. She loved hearing about that and wanted to know every detail of colour and texture and taste. But then she got sad that I was spending so much time out and she began to protest about me walking back late, alone in the dark, especially on winter evenings. So I told her how Yolanda always stuck up for me at school, keeping me with her in the playground, even when she was with the older girls. When I said how kind her family were, making me feel happy in their home, she just closed her eyes, as if remembering her own, and said softly, "You go, child. Make the most of it." And after that no more was said, although she was always waiting on the area steps for my return.

Yolanda taught me the most important lesson of my life. She taught me not to be ashamed of being different

Her family taught me something else—something that was to define my future. They showed me that there was a world outside the one I knew, a bigger, brighter world, full of colour and excitement. And better still, a life full of emotions they were not afraid to feel and passions they were eager to explore.

As my world expanded, Cornelius' shrank. In the end there was only the bottle and he drowned in it. He drank more and more. We never saw him in the evenings now until he was brought home insensible, by one or other of his drinking buddies, sometimes complete strangers who had found him in the street. Gradually, he became an object of pity and contempt rather than fear and that suited me fine.

Mother said nothing. She looked after him when she could and left him well alone when she could not. In the end, she attempted to talk to him. She picked one morning soon after he had lost his job. He sat, bleary eyed with a yellowish tinge, at the kitchen table, unable to raise his cup of tea to his lips with his shaking hands. For once, she did not attempt to help him, but watched, stony-faced, as he spilled most of it down the front of his shirt. He was a sad sight now, his good looks gone. His eyes were blood-shot, his face puffy and blotched with the angry red rash that used to be euphemistically called 'grog blossoms'. He had formerly been a rather dapper man, vain of his looks and fussy about his clothes. He had also been fastidious in his habits and very clean. Now he no longer cared. His stained shirt had no collar (they were detachable in those days) and he wore a greasy looking scarf around his neck. His trousers were crumpled and creased and there was an tear in the knee. He hadn't shaved and he smelled awful.

Mother weighed in a way she would never have dared before. "You're killing yourself. You know that, don't you?"

"And if I am who would care?"

The tears came easily to him now. He seemed to exist in a watery world of self-pity. Indeed, he relished it, wallowing. He seemed to me like the papier-mâché we made at school, steeped too long in liquid, a sodden amorphous mass, no longer anything.

"And whose fault is that?" Her tone was more strict than angry.

He looked accusingly at her. "You never loved me."

What could she say? There was no reply to that. It was true. She had only ever pitied him, and too many blows had broken that.

For a moment they looked at each other in silence across the kitchen table. The exhausted battle ground of their marriage. He rose unsteadily, and for a fleeting moment he was oddly dignified. In *vino veritas* indeed. Then he looked down at his congealing breakfast and you could see it made his stomach churn. He retched and vomited up a thin trail of frothy bile. His moment gone, he shuffled painfully towards the door and then went out. We never saw him again.

Late that night a policeman knocked on our door. Cornelius had collapsed in the bar of 'The Windsor Castle'. The landlord had called an ambulance, but he never regained consciousness. They took him to St Mary Abbotts hospital where it was recorded that he was dead on arrival.

Mother took the news stoically. But she was pale and shaken. She sat up most of the night by the fire in Mrs Lomasney's chair. I stayed with her the next day and we went to the hospital to get the certificate and then to the Town Hall to register the death. I thought how strange it was that our messy lives were book ended in this way by officialdom, scraps of paper to mark the living from the dead, and brand us bastard or widow.

In truth, all I felt was a kind of solemn relief. But as we turned back into Peel Street on our way home and Mother had still not spoken, I tried to reach her. I told her I was sorry she was a widow.

She shook her head. "No, you're not and neither am I."

She stuffed the key resolutely in the door lock and turned it. "He should have died in the war. He never really survived it."

We went in and I shut the door behind us. And that was that. She had lumped him together with all the other pain and loss she had suffered from that conflict and turned her back on it. She wasn't one for introspection. She got on with life, my mother. A life that was far more pleasant now that it had been before. The house was hers—he had left it to her in his will—and after what she called "a decent interval" she put aside her black and went out and embraced her life. She got herself a job in a small restaurant in Notting Hill Gate, 'The Litten Tree' it was called. She worked hard and did well. She started out as a waitress, but was soon promoted to Manageress. She made friends and occasionally invited them to our home. Our gatherings lacked the careless joie de vivre of the Barronis; by comparison they were sedate and a bit stilted, tea and cake, scones and homemade jam rather than wine and song, but the sad, fear-filled house was beginning to be a home, ours, and if our first steps were hesitant, we were still stumbling out of the shadows and into a brighter life.

Chapter Four

I had grown to like school. After the initial Calvary, it all settled down and I found I liked the disciplined day-to-day order. Its cloistered certainty reassured me. We were very well-taught; our teachers stern but scholarly, all rather forbidding maiden graduates, "blue stockings" we called them, but it was impossible not to respect their learning and the love they had for it. Although I eventually balked at some of the sillier rules, I loved to study and found that I was nearly always somewhere near the top of the class. Never the top but very close to it and through this I was accorded a kind of status that had nothing to with birth and that made me happy.

Yolanda left school a year before I did. Matriculating with honours, as we all knew she would. She went to work straight away, working for a friend of her father's who ran the Waldorf Hotel in the Aldwych. Overnight, she changed from a schoolgirl with ribbons in her hair and a shapeless old blazer to a smart young woman, who wore a two piece suit, a costume we called it then, to go to business. She wore make-up now, sporting bright red lips and nails and had her hair cut into a stylish bob. She looked wonderful, but very different. I used to meet her after work; I felt an awful clod, lumbering along beside her with my satchel and school shoes and socks. She was a young lady and I was still a child. I felt the difference keenly. She took no notice whatsoever: despite her allegiance to chic, Yolanda paid no heed to other people's appearance. At least, she never judged them by it.

Predictably I hated school without her. I had never really made friends with the Agathas and Deidres that were my classmates. We had learned to tolerate each other, but it was no more than that. I worked with a vengeance, getting put up a year so that I could leave as soon as possible. I knew there was absolutely no chance of my going to university. My form teacher had mentioned it, suggesting she put me forward for the Oxbridge entrance exams with a view perhaps to a scholarship; but my mother looked ashen when I told her, and said she was only just managing as things were and that she was "hanging on" to the house by the skin of her teeth, waiting for the day when my wages, whatever they were, would come as a welcome relief. So that was that. She had never told me before. I knew that I would have to do everything I could to help her. I told Yolanda and she said briskly not to mind because what she called "the real world" was far more exciting than a sort of "extended school" which was what she imagined a women's college would be. She may have had a point, although I noticed that a lot of her new friends were university students. But then they were mostly male. Yolanda in her new guise was a man magnet. Men fell at her feet, making awful fools of themselves, staring at her with a silly fixed smile, opening doors, helping her down from the bus and offering to carry her bags. She turned them all down with scorn, which oddly enough, only seemed to make them more ardent. It was very peculiar. I told Mother and she laughed and then added a bit grimly that she was "not at all surprised; that was the Latin in her" and I should watch out for it in me. I knew she was thinking of Jaime again, so I went upstairs to struggle with my irregular verbs.

In what was to become a pattern in my life, I listened to Mother's advice, but didn't take it. Yolanda introduced me to her new friends who all seemed to be students and intellectuals. Pipe-smoking young men in Oxford bags and corduroy jackets. Very left-wing and avant-garde. It was all very exciting. I spent Saturday and Sunday afternoons, tricked up in an old green dress of Yolanda's, a smear of lipstick and sprinkling of powder, in bedsitting rooms in Earls Court and Bloomsbury where the tea was stewed and the red wine corrosive. They talked at length about Politics and Art and Freedom. All the important things in life had capital letters it seemed. They argued with passion and interrupted a lot. Not always politely.

But this was adult life, or so I thought, and as such, despite the often filthy surroundings (the intelligentsia didn't go in for cleaning apparently) the gas ring in the corner and the loo shared by many, it had an enchantment and a lure that was irresistible. I hardly spoke at these gatherings because I didn't want anyone to ask me what I did and find out I was still at school. But once an eager young man, with Brillianteened locks and only a few pimples, offered to walk me home and I became giddy with the prospect of what my life could be. He was rather sweet. His name was Ronald Hughes and he worked in insurance in the city. But he was "political" he said and supported the Republicans in Spain. I didn't know who they were so I just nodded, looking serious. He wanted to buy me a drink on the way home but I didn't feel I could get away with that, so I turned him down. He looked genuinely disappointed which gave me another thrill. The power of it, you see. Then he said he hoped he would see me again. I rushed in and shut the door before Mother could see him. I was thrilled to bits. The glow of that evening lasted for nearly a week. Perhaps it was the Latin in me.

When the euphoria of that evening began to die down, and I stopped walking to the bus stop dreaming I was Greta Garbo in floor length white chiffon, waltzing 'til dawn in a vast empty room full of dry ice and Ronald Colman, the chill of reality began to impinge.

I had never imagined Mother had money worries. To be fair, she had never indicated to me by so much as a frown or a pursed lip that she had. I just assumed that since Cornelius was gone and she had the house, our troubles were over. It had never occurred to me that she might struggle to maintain us on her very modest wage. We lived so frugally—never treats or outings, or fancy gifts at Christmas or birthdays. Our idea of a good time was a cup of tea and a current bun in Lyons Corner House or rifling through the remnant counter at Swan & Edgar. I never thought she was struggling. In short, I never thought. I was far too preoccupied with my own daydreams.

I felt sick when I realised how little I had thought of her. She was always so capable, so effective—the notion she might need help, even mine, had never once crossed my mind. I confided all this to Yolanda one wintry Saturday afternoon in a sudden rush of tears and mounting shame. Yolanda hugged me, then set about finding the solution. She asked me if I wanted to go to university and when I said firmly that was not an option, she said if I only wanted to matriculate I should ask if I could take the exams a year early. I would have to matriculate, she said, because then I would get a better job. I would surely pass, she went on airily, especially with her help, and then I could leave school and get a good job to help my mother. She made it all sound very simple.

So, on Monday morning after prayers, briefed by Yolanda as if I were appearing before a High Court judge, I made an appointment to see the Head Mistress during the lunch break.

Duly at half past one, my hastily swallowed stew and dumplings lying like rocks in my stomach, I stood before the Inner Sanctum (which was what we called the HM's office) and knocked at the door.

"Come" was the imperious response. I entered and shut the door behind me. HM's (as in Her Majesty's) office was a large, surprisingly light room with a handsome marble fireplace in which a cosy fire blazed, bookcases full of important looking books and a huge desk that stretched right across the room like an altar. The sacrificial kind. There was only one chair. Sitting was only for HM, mere mortals had to stand.

She was seated at her desk writing. She did not look up. I approached the desk with trepidation, not daring to get too close. I stood and waited, one side of me roasting in too close proximity to the fire, the other shivering in the draft from the open window. It seemed a terrible extravagance to me, a roaring fire in a room with an open window, burning all that coal only to be cold. My mother would never have allowed it.

I waited for what seemed like hours, listening to the traffic on the road outside, wishing I were in it. There was no sound in the room except the crackling of the fire and the scratching of her pen on the paper. Eventually, she stopped writing, put her pen down, read over what she had written, then screwed the lid on the pen and put it down on the silver pen tray in front of her. Then and only then, all other possibilities exhausted, did she look at me.

"Well, Jewanitaah" (she dragged out every syllable of my name from the harsh initial j to the long final a as if to emphasize its outlandishness) She was called Janet—a rough tweed skirt of a name, robust and durable.

"What is it?" Her eyes glinted behind her glasses, cold and grey as stones. She had very little time for me, despite my good marks.

"I... er," now I came to it, Yolanda's coaching fled and I didn't know what to say. She raised her eyebrows and let me have the full power of her basilisk stare. Men have died of fright for less. Terrified as a rabbit in a car's headlights, I abandoned Yolanda's rather convoluted speech and plunged right in while I could still breathe.

"I need to help my mother."

She looked even more severe, if that was possible, pulling down her mouth and pursing her lips.

"Yes." And then a pause that seemed to last for years.

"I imagine you do. I seem to recall your domestic situation is..." Here words failed her, as if nothing in her vocabulary could express anything so foul.

"... irregular." She seemed genuinely pleased to have found a word that would relieve her of the need to consider the reality of a bastard child and a single parent.

"I was wondering..."

"What were you wondering?" Her expression was utterly closed, it was a fortress of a face, shuttered and impregnable. Did she really imagine I was going to ask her for help? The absurdity of that made me smile. The grim humour of it set me free.

"I need to work to help my mother. So I was hoping that I could matriculate early... if I worked really hard..."

We both knew failure was inconceivable. The honour of the school was at stake.

"I see." She considered the possibility. But not for long.

"I don't see why not. Your marks are good enough and if you work really hard, I see no reason why you should not achieve an adequate result."

We both knew I was much better than that. But no regret was expressed at my not being able to continue my studies, although I was easily good enough to.

She nodded a sort of dismissal. "I will speak to Miss James and make the necessary arrangements."

She looked back down at her papers.

"You may go."

"Thank you." I made for the door, grateful for escape. As I turned the door knob, the sound of her voice stopped me in my tracks.

"Jewanitaah, your concern for your parent (emphasizing the singular)... does you credit."

To my horror, tears stung my eyes. I turned away so that she could not see my face. That was the first and only kind remark ever made to me in that school. I opened the door and went out.

I worked like a maniac for the next school year. Every evening when I was not being crammed by Yolanda, whose idea was to stuff me full of facts like a foie gras goose, I sat up until all hours at the kitchen table, sustained by black coffee and Abernethy biscuits, cramming in even more and doing old exam papers until I could reel off reams of History, Geography, General Science, Eng Lit et al with the dispatch of a tap dancer performing a rather snappy routine.

I read somewhere that Ginger Rogers had once executed a particular dance routine with such speed and brio that the feathers flew off her dress. I felt like that then: if I moved I would moult facts.

Mother was worried. She told me I was "pushing myself too hard." She fussed around me, making my favourite foods and muttering about bedtime. I took no notice. I was desperate for escape and matric was my ticket out. Consequently, I went for it with the subtlety of an express train—full tilt, non-stop.

The only recreation I allowed myself during that year were the books on India I took out of the library. They were my treat when the study was done. I read in bed at night. I stopped going to social gatherings with Yolanda. We both agreed that would be a distraction, and besides I could pick up those threads after the exam. So my only refuge was India. Slowly I devoured all the books in the library on the subject—from romantic fiction to agricultural reports. India fascinated me: the immensity of its landscape, the diversity of its peoples. The power and wealth of the princes, the grinding poverty of the lower castes, all cheek by jowl, held me in thrall.

It still does. But then it was the stuff of my thoughts by day and my dreams by night. A world of different peoples and their Gods, another way of being. I longed to go there. But I confided these feelings to no one, certainly not to Mother and not even to Yolanda. I was far too afraid they'd laugh at me.

Eventually, one chilly morning in June when the thin grey rain fell like arrows outside, I walked into the main hall with its oak panelling and honour boards, ponderous and stuffed to paralysis with facts, sat down at the desk with my number on it and turned over my first exam paper. I put my head down and prayed that I could regurgitate everything I had learned in a coherent and rational manner. For a split second the print on the papers swam before my eyes and I thought I would faint. Then I pulled myself together. If I failed now I would be stuck here, an object of ridicule and a lesson in hubris. I dredged up my mother in me, breathed deeply, read the question and began to write.

Eight exams and two weeks later, I emerged into the pale sunlight of early summer. I still wore my jersey, but I could feel the sun's warmth on my back. I didn't stay to mull over the questions, their unfairness and the inadequacy of our answers with my fellow sufferers, but ran for the bus, headlong and free. It was too late to worry now, and besides, I had worried so much before the exams, I had somehow exhausted my capacity for angst. Now it was over and I was glad. Whatever the outcome. I had decided that in the dreadful event of my failure, I would leave school anyway and get a job in a shop or be a Nippy in a Lyons Corner House. You couldn't need Trigonometry or Latin for that. No, childhood and shame were done with, I decided. I ran to embrace adult life. The world looked as if it were brand new to me that afternoon. The sky washed clean by the long rainy spring, the leaves on the trees a bright, tender green. All London was mine, full of life and promise. My life was about to begin and I was determined to leave behind everything that had caused me pain. As an adult I could face other adults as an equal, not a guilty secret. I could look them straight in the eye and lie, if need be. It was none of their business anyway. They need never know. And that way, I could forget.

In the coming weeks I transformed myself. I went to Mama B and said, "I want to look like Yolanda. You know, grown up. Smart." She smiled.

Yolanda scowled. "You never will with that hair. You can't be grown up with plaits."

I saw her point, so I begged Mama B to cut my hair. At first she demurred. When I undid my plaits, she brushed my hair and frowned.

"It's a pity. Such lovely hair." Then she looked stern. "What did your Mama say?" Yolanda and I looked at each other. "You have asked her, haven't you?"

"Of course she has." Yolanda lied. Then she opened the drawer and took out the scissors.

So Mama Barroni cut my hair into a sleek bob just like Yolanda's. As my heavy black locks fell onto the floor, I felt light, relieved of a burden. I shook my new short locks out. Mama B then waved it for me, using sugar water and Marcel grips. My mother cried when she first saw me. "Your beautiful hair" she wept. Then she got cross. "I spent years looking after that hair. You should have consulted me." But I couldn't because I knew what her response would be. And I was right. I took very little notice of Mother now; I knew if I were to take my place in a grown up world, I could not remain her timid, silent child.

Yolanda gave me some of her clothes and make-up, and her father pulled strings with his many acquaintances and got me a job. A really good job at the Waldorf. With Yolanda. I cried when he told me that. He told me I would start in the office, making tea and filing, but then he patted me awkwardly when I tried to thank him and said although I was starting at the bottom of the ladder, he was sure I wouldn't stay there. Then he mentioned the wage he had arranged for me. It seemed a fortune, exceeding both my mother's and Yolanda's wages. Yolanda began to protest but he frowned at her, his thick black brows forming a stern line across his forehead, and he said merely, "Her wages are not her own. She helps her mama, Yolanda." And Yolanda shut up and nodded at me, trying hard not to resent it.

After a few weeks of uneasy idleness at home the results came through. I had passed in all subjects with distinction in English and History.

Chapter Five

Mama and Papa Barroni decided to hold a supper party in my honour to celebrate my success. They insisted on inviting Mother. I viewed the prospect with dread. The meeting of two worlds: I couldn't see how they would mesh and it caused me quite a few sleepless nights. Chalk and cheese. Mama B must have had an inkling of how I might feel because she had sent the invitation by post, intuiting correctly that if I were entrusted with it, it might well not arrive. Mother looked a bit alarmed at first, but said firmly, "how kind," and wrote back at once to accept.

So one evening a week or so later, sitting politely in her grey flannel skirt and best white blouse (the one with the tatting lace trim) her feet neatly crossed at the ankles and removed for once from her own surroundings, Mother suddenly seemed small and very much alone amid the bustling brouhaha of the Barroni family

She declined the glass of red wine the rest of us had and

instead was given sherry. She liked a sweet sherry, but the Barronis only had dry. At the first sip she seemed thrown, a little daunted even, but she soon pulled herself together. Elizabeth Bruce was not a woman to be beaten by a glass of sherry. She sipped at it daintily, remarked on its quality and joined in. She was game, my ma.

Mama Barroni smiled and beamed, showering me with approval. She was genuinely proud of me, but her flowery response made all others seem understated, even niggardly. Papa B toasted my success and insisted we all stand to drink to my future. You could see Mother was utterly phased, and even more so when Mama B produced a gift.

"For you, cara, to make you even more beautiful," she handed me a small white and gold box. Inside it was a pair of gold and pearl earrings—they were perfect, elegant and expensive. I thanked her and she enfolded me in her operatic embrace. Mother stood by awkwardly.

"How very kind..." she ventured, but her quiet voice was drowned out by the whole clan singing "for she's a jolly good fellow" at full pelt. They could raise the roof, the Barroni family in full song. Mama B grabbed my hands and danced me round, Yolanda stamped and cheered, Papa whistled and clapped and Mother stood amazed, wondering what on earth was going on.

You could tell she was uneasy. Her face wore an anxious frown and a tight look around the mouth. She was unhappy with this avalanche of feelings. Especially her own. She felt outclassed, competing for her child. I could see she was torn between maternal love, possessive and proprietorial, and her cast iron sense of what was right.

She needn't have worried. There was never any competition. Mama and Papa Barroni were wonderful people and I loved them dearly. They gave me warmth, colour and laughter at a time when my life had none of these things. But there was never any question as to who I would long for. For the rest of my life—in all places and at all times, hers was the face I would long to see. Her calm, wry smile, the premature lines on her still youthful face, the touch of her cool, work-worn hands (she always claimed they were the secret of her amazingly light pastry—cold hands). She could hold back all the harm in the world. Only her. No one else even came close. Though it was a very long time before I would admit it.

"You'll have to get your ears pierced," she said, as the rumpus died down. She sounded almost regretful as if this was yet another closing door on my childhood. She took one out of the box and held it up to look at it closely. "They're beautiful pearls," she stared at their tear shaped lustre, knowing she would never possess jewellery like this. "You make sure you take care of them." She smiled at Mama B, not quite able to look her in the eye. Then she sat down. She looked older somehow. At last acknowledging that life had not been kind to her, that she had not been loved as she had loved.

Beside her, Mama B all generous curves in claret

coloured silk, with glittering diamonds at her ears and throat, seemed overflowing with the largesse life had showered on her. Her lovely home, her loving, squabbling family, her food and wine, flowers and porcelain, the frail, translucent Virgin Mary on the wall and the heavy silver candle sticks on the table, all of it formed a cornucopia with herself at the centre, and my mother to one side, a little brown sparrow beside a bird of paradise.

Mother was very quiet on the bus on the way home after the party. In fact, during the weekend that followed we hardly spoke at all. I was too wrapped up in preparing my meagre wardrobe (mostly borrowed from Yolanda) for my first day at work and dreaming about my adult life and she? Who ever really knew what she thought or felt? She was never one to admit to feelings, let alone discuss them and so they remained forever unspoken—a vast, undiscovered swathe of isolation that put miles between us.

Mother could be distant and even remote when she chose to be, but her support for me was never in doubt. It was the constant of my childhood and, as I learned far too late, the bedrock of my whole existence. Years later, I realised she was simply the best friend I ever had.

Before I started work, she sold the gold pin Mrs Lomasney had given her on her wedding day. I don't suppose it held very happy memories for her, but it was a pretty thing, a gold filigree spray of flowers, and about the only piece of real jewellery she ever owned.

Anyway, she sold it and the first I knew of it was when

she announced that we would be going to Swan and Edgar the following morning to buy me a "costume for business." We had a lovely day together, choosing this suit, eventually plumping for a black barathea with two white silk blouses to match. Mother pronounced it "smart and practical" and suggested that I could ring the changes later on and buy blouses in other colours. I was thrilled with this suit, convinced its elegant severity turned me instantly into a grown up. I showed them off proudly to Yolanda, who approved of the blouses but raised an eyebrow when shown the suit, "Going to a funeral?" she said. My face fell. Had we chosen something completely wrong? After all, what did either of us know about business? And Mother had taken such care and spent all her money on it.

"Is it wrong? Do I look silly?" I could hardly breathe I was so upset.

"Of course not, you big dope. It's very chic and you look beautiful. Because you are beautiful. How can anyone as bright as you be such a fool?"

She looked skyward with her arms in a broad gesture of application, appealing to the heavens. Then she walked round me, sizing me up. Suit, idiocy and all.

"Drop dead gorgeous. Just a bit sombre, that's all. Come on, let's go, we're late!" As ever, we were going to the Barronis for supper. As I put my treasure carefully back in the wardrobe, she smiled and said gently.

"One day we'll dress you in scarlet."

We walked straight into the latest Barroni family feud. Over dinner, as usual.

Uncle Vittorio (Mama's brother) owned a restaurant. It appeared that he had been buying his Parmesan elsewhere. This was treachery, it was almost tantamount to treason.

"I did everything for that man. I gave him money... I found him premises..." Papa declaimed. I was sure he had. He was absolutely furious. Mama was distraught.

"My brother... my own flesh and blood..." she appealed to thin air in his absence, "I named my first born child after you..."

Her manner was histrionic, but her distress was real. I hated to see her so upset. Papa stood up, pale and dignified and laid aside his napkin. He hadn't touched his food. "I never want to hear that man's name again. Do you understand me?"

"Gonna be a bit tricky, since you called your son after him," Yolanda began to clear the table. She was used to this. She took it all in her stride. But I was appalled. My Mother's fate lead me to take such threats very seriously.

Mama burst into tears. Papa left the room. He went into the little room by the pantry he used as an office and slammed the door. After a few minutes silence, the mournful strains of Verdi's Requiem billowed out. Mama stopped crying, and rested her elbows on the table, listening to the music. I thought only the Barronis would insist that a gramophone be an essential part of an office. They taught me so much. That life is full of crises and conflict and the timeless consolation of art. I loved them very much.

The morning of my first day at work, Mother made me a hearty breakfast of eggs and bacon and toast. I didn't want it, I was so nervous, my stomach was jumping up and down in a most peculiar manner and I actually felt a bit sick, but I knew she would stand over me 'til I ate it, so I forced down as much of it as I could, then put on my jacket, clumsily dabbed powder across my face and turned to face her for the first time as an equal. She looked at me, unsmiling, then said softly, "You're a bonnie lass, no mistake." And I kissed her and ran before either of us crumbled.

It was a cold, wet day, not like summer at all, but I didn't care. I wasn't going to be outside. From the moment I entered the hotel by the grand revolving doors (my first mistake, not using the staff entrance at the rear) and walked across the vast marble lobby with its glittering chandeliers and heavy, silk drapes, I felt I was in different world. Actually, I was. Everything in the Waldorf was designed to provide an insulating, luxurious comfort; an opulent paradise for the privileged. The unrelenting harshness of the city outside, its clamour and grime had no place in there. The Waldorf was a playground for adults, a place where all wishes were granted, provided you could pay for them.

I was put to work in a small back office that lead out of the General Manager's suite of offices where Yolanda worked. I was shown a mountain of jumbled papers, piled precariously high on a desk and given some basic instructions in filing. The manager's assistant, a young man called Freddy, showed me what to do and said to ask him or Yolanda if I got stuck. But Yolanda was nowhere to be seen. She was "in a meeting," he said. So off I went. It was a simple enough system, all perfectly obvious. There was just an awful lot of it. So I worked away, anxious to make good, only dimly aware when Yolanda stuck her head round the door and said, "Got you breaking rocks already, have they?" I nodded but didn't really look up. I was being paid a very good wage and I was determined to earn it.

After what seemed like a short while, but was in fact two hours, Freddy came in with a tray. On it was a small pot of coffee, a white and gold cup and saucer with the hotel monogram, a jug of hot milk and two, tiny thin biscuits. He said they were called "tuiles" but they looked like baby Abernethys, which was fine by me. They were delicious and so was the strong and fragrant coffee. It all seemed very grand to me.

I didn't dare stop working, but looked up and thanked Freddy. He hung around in the doorway, obviously wanting to talk, then he said it was coffee break now and he would bring his through to have with me as it was my first day. He made it all seem like a great favour and I felt duly grateful. He explained that Yolanda had her coffee with the General Manager. It seemed there was a definite hierarchy to these things. He sat down and drank his coffee while I drank mine, talking away about this and that and I slowly began to realise I was being chatted up. I was thrilled at being part of such an adult exchange. I flirted back a bit, but not too much because I didn't know the rules of the game. It was clear there were some. So I took it all very gingerly, careful of every move, a bit like ice-skating for the first time, terrified that one false step, one clumsy aside would land me back in the world of a lonely child, feeling silly and sore.

In any case, I didn't really like him in that way. He was pale, slight and colourless, with sparse blond hair, already thinning on top, and pasty looking skin. But he was trying to be funny and friendly, and I was pleased and excited that any grown up man, however substandard, would bother with me at all.

I confided as much to Yolanda. She took me out to lunch that first day, to the nearest ABC for a sandwich, explaining that normally we would go to the staff canteen on the fifth floor, which was very good and also free. She said she wanted to "put me straight. About Freddy." That sounded a bit ominous so I asked her why. And as she smoked several of her squashed up cigarettes, "Passing Clouds" she called them, she offered me one and then came baldly to the point.

"Don't encourage him," she said and I felt bad because I knew I probably had. I started a half-hearted defence.

"He tries it on with everyone. He's not fussy." I was a bit crestfallen at that.

"He's not good enough for you." She inhaled deeply. "But he is your boss. Well, certainly your senior. So don't piss him off. Not yet, anyway."

Then she smiled at me and launched into a detailed description of the latest developments in the Barroni family feud, of which there were many. I pitched in as always in my place as outside observer and together we went through the ramifications of the latest row until it was time to go back to work. They were a sort of operatic Forsyte Saga—the Barroni family—with their feuds, and bitter disputes and tearful reunions that endured through generations and were a huge source of conversational fascination to us both. A kind of permanent on-going drama, in which only the names of the protagonists changed—the themes were always the same. Love, money, family. All things I knew absolutely nothing about. It was very consoling somehow.

Then we went back to work. I saved my afternoon tea biscuit to take home to Mother. When I handed it to her, she bit into it cautiously. I had wrapped it up in a clean handkerchief and it had crumbled a little in my bag, leaving a thin dusty trail on the lining. She nodded approvingly, her mouth full. "Not bad," she said and that was praise from Mother.

Chapter Six

At the end of my first week, the General Manager came to speak to me. He walked into my cubby hole of an office, past the seemingly endless mountains of unfiled papers still piled high, manoeuvred his way rather gracefully past two broken chairs and stood in front of me on the other side of the desk. He was a plump pigeon of a man, in pinstriped trousers and a grey silk tie, with a modest paunch and soft podgy hands that were oddly feminine. I stood up as I would have done at school, but he waved a lordly hand and said it looked like I had made "a good start." Then he compressed his mouth and double chins into what could have been a smile. I wasn't sure. He was so grand I almost felt I should curtsey. But then I looked up and saw Freddy, standing behind him pulling a face exactly like his boss and he looked so silly, I smiled involuntarily. The GM, as all his staff called him, was apparently satisfied with this response, because he compressed his lower face still more, causing his chins to form pleats of flesh driven into his stiff collar. It looked painful. Then he swept out. I felt pleased and relieved. For a long time approval of any kind from almost any source caused me to feel absurdly grateful.

I was even more pleased when later that afternoon, the chief clerk came round and left a small, square manila envelope on my desk. It had my name on it and felt bulky. Inside I found my wages slip with all the deductions clearly marked and more money than I had ever had in my life. Three whole pounds.

On my way home that night I bought Mother a bunch of anemones and a pineapple. I knew she loved both and never had either. I had never tried fresh pineapple, only the tinned kind at Christmas, but she had told me about it. I burst into the kitchen and plonked the flowers, fruit and my wages down on the table in front of her. She examined them all in silence, then raised one hand to her face.

"Oh Jeannie," she said (she always called me that, especially when she was pleased with me, leaving my full name for punishment purposes only, as if it were too grand and elaborate for every day use) Then she smiled broadly and said I was a naughty girl and I shouldn't have, but she was a bit flushed and a stray tear ran down into her mouth and betrayed her.

She told me to put the kettle on while she put the flowers in water. She loved anemones, arranging them with the care and delight others would have given roses.

She placed them proudly in the centre of the table and announced we would have some of the pineapple for pudding tonight. To celebrate my first week at work.

Then she opened the wage packet and counted the money out on the table, she took two pounds and ten shillings and slid the remainder across the table to me. It wasn't much out of three pounds but it still seemed like a fortune to me. And it was too, because I hadn't any expenses except for my bus fare, which was only pennies. All my lunches were free, courtesy of the Waldorf staff canteen, which was very good indeed. So the rest was 'pin money'.

It was odd working in a hotel. Like school, it was a world within the wider one. Isolated by its glamour and its ethos, dedicated to the comfort of others. It had its own laws and customs, its own rigid pecking order, its own particular joys and heartbreak. The nerve centre of this mini cosmos was the GM's office. He ran the whole show with the precision of a Swiss watch, making sure that the Herculean labour of supply and demand of all services required ran with seemingly effortless ease. Except it didn't, it only appeared to.

Behind the scenes he fielded an endless stream of complaints from chambermaids and duchesses, the tearful vapours of the Head Housekeeper who kept a steely, grey clad exterior but would crack alarmingly when criticised; to the Head Chef who would rampage his way, bellowing from his kingdom in the kitchen if the fish was not fresh or his soufflés collapsed when kept waiting. He was French you see, Freddy said, as if that explained everything. "Got high standards." "So does my mother," I replied, "but she makes less noise." I'd never heard anything like it. The Barronis were child's play compared to him. Chef was a human roller coaster of a man. Charming and avuncular when all went well, he would bring us samples of his most delicious dishes to try, but when angry he raged and yelled with a vigour that exhausted those around him. The sous chefs looked like pallid little ghosts in their white outfits with their white terrified faces, hardly daring to breathe in case they got something wrong. He also said "*Salaud*" a lot, which was water off a duck's back to us because we didn't understand what it meant, even the GM who would proudly claim he had been trained at the Ritz in Paris. Except he hadn't as it turned out, but we only found that out much later, though his lack of French comprehension should have given us a clue. Yolanda, however, did understand and she didn't like it. She explained why to me one late shopping evening after work when, exhausted from trying on the clothes we could never buy, we consoled ourselves with poached eggs on toast at Lyons Corner House.

"Unfair advantage," she said, as she spread butter thickly on her toast.

"What?" I asked, my mouth full of egg.

"Swearing in a language you know the recipient won't understand."

"Oh."

She took a mouthful of tea. "Cowardly, don't you think? Getting a dig in when you know you won't get one back?"

I smiled at her, thinking how wonderful she was. She was always ready for combat, Yolanda, but she believed in a fair fight.

I quickly fitted into the hotel hierarchy—and though I never accepted Freddy's repeated offer of a drink after work, I often sat and chatted with him in the cafeteria. He was a bit keen, I think, but easily rebuffed and never one to take offence. He flirted with everyone, just as Yolanda had said, and although I probably interested him because I didn't take him up on his offer, as others did, he wasn't going to lose any sleep over it. And more remarkably, nor would he let it sour our working relationship, which was a very good thing because we were always in each others' pockets, work-wise.

It was a bit more difficult to navigate my way around the ardour of the GM. He liked me because it soon became obvious that I was hard-working and reliable. I was also far too bright for the job (modesty apart!) so he could safely entrust me with tasks he should have taken care of himself. He needed that because his job was so demanding, he was often genuinely exhausted. He liked to delegate where possible, he said, to give the youngsters a chance. He also liked young girls, especially if they were pretty. The chambermaids were often found weeping in the staff ladies, having discovered they could not refuse his clumsy advances. Those who did were deemed negligent of their duties and swiftly fired. Evidently he felt a hand up the skirt or a caress of a young woman's breast was part of his *droit de seigneur* as Hotel Supremo. I doubt he did more, however, and he did nothing at all with me. Well, only once.

That day he had stood in the doorway to my office, staring in a fixed way and breathing hard as I pulled my skirt up over my knees to stand on a chair, which was the only way I could reach the upper shelves to stack the files. He made a move towards me and I was helpless. Trapped with both arms full, outstretched, and balanced precariously on the chair, I felt his hand slide right up my leg and start to caress my thigh. I couldn't even move out of range. Then a strangled snort stopped him dead. Yolanda stood in the doorway like the wrath of God. I thought she was going to start breathing fire. The hand slid limply back down my leg and he moved away as she glared at him with real loathing

He withered before her gaze, knowing that although she was very much his junior, her contacts in the business could make him unemployable if she chose to get malicious. I doubt the truth would have done much harm, but she was perfectly capable of cooking up a tale to ruin him, and they both knew it. He scurried back into his office like a cockroach caught in a bright light.

I shook a bit and the chair rocked dangerously.

"This the first time?"

I nodded and the chair shook. "Get down. If he tries anything again, tell me."

"I don't think he will."

"No, neither do I." She turned to go. "Close your mouth. You look simple."

You could only really obey Yolanda when she got like this. Born to command. But she was a very good friend. He never went near me again.

Mother was very anxious about me working in a hotel, especially at first, because of her own experience. She didn't have to labour the point. She just said, "Be very careful, Jeannie. People aren't always what you think they are." And she looked so sad when she said that that I knew she was thinking of my father and I cursed him again for his attentions to her and his abandonment of me.

However, I was torn because if he hadn't pursued her with such ardour, I wouldn't have been here at all, and my life was starting to be so good, I couldn't honestly regret that. It was just getting the balance right, I used to ponder as I strap hung in the crowded bus on the way home, between the joy of flirting with the opposite sex and the awful consequences of getting caught out.

Slowly, I was pulling out of the shadow of my childhood and starting to see myself in a different light. Yolanda and her family had always told me I was good looking, but I just thought they were being kind. I couldn't see it myself. You could see why. I was too thin, too tall, with eyes and mouth too big for my face and feet too big for everything.

But when I left school and ceased to be the bastard girl with the outlandish name, I began to flourish. The anonymity of adult life suited me very well. No one worried about my provenance now. Another perhaps even more tyrannous hierarchy took over. I began to use make-up and fix my hair. I spent all my pin money on clothes. And although I played safe, aiming for elegance rather than man appeal, I began to be noticed. Men looked at me in the street, and even I could not mistake the admiration in their eyes. Doors were opened and packages carried, conversations were begun, a hand shake would be held for too long. Some women stared at me with what may have been envy. Shop assistants sighed when I bought the clothes I had tried on and told me wistfully "it could have been made for you." This sudden attention went to my head like wine. After years of insignificance and opprobrium, I was sought after, desired even. I could not get enough of it.

I began to cultivate my image. Yolanda took me to have my ears pierced one Saturday afternoon after work. We stopped at lunchtime on Saturdays in those days. We went to a swanky department store in Oxford Street. The least said about it the better. Yolanda had promised me it wouldn't hurt. She lied. My eyes were watering for quite some time afterwards, but when the soreness died down, the earrings Mama B had given me looked lovely. You have to suffer to be beautiful, Yolanda said sternly, it was just a good thing she hadn't told me how much.

A few weeks later I went to her hairdressers in Drury Lane. Madame Andrea, she was called, who operated in a tiny shop that was all padded pink silk and gilt fittings. It was a bit like being inside a very expensive box of chocolates. She wrapped me in a cape and sat me down, staring at me in the mirror. Yes, she said at last, now I see. I was too scared to ask her what she saw.

I just sat there, closed my eyes and hoped for the best. She trimmed my hair and then told me I had to have a perm because my hair was so straight and heavy, it would not "hold a curl" any other way. So she doused me in an evil-smelling solution, that made my eyes water, rolled my hair up tightly in metal clips and left me to stew. After what seemed like hours when even vanity and hope could not distract me from the fear of all my hair falling out and being left bald as a boiled egg, I was rinsed and shampooed and then my hair, which to my huge relief seemed to have survived the ordeal, was "styled" and I sat beneath a metal dome that felt like a blast furnace until I was pronounced cooked. Then red-faced and anxious, I watched as my hair was brushed out.

I nearly wept with relief. Madame Andrea brushed the sides up and away from my face and the rest fell in neat black curls around my head. Then she stood back, exhausted from her labours, but smiling and triumphant. When I put my earrings back on even I could see that I looked very good indeed. I had never looked this good in my life.

"You must always wear your hair like this." And so I did for nigh on twenty years. However silly her pretensions, Madame Andrea had divined exactly what would flatter my face most. Suddenly, my eyes looked huge, my mouth soft and shapely and the whole shape of my face and head had acquired an elegance and poise I had never dreamt of. She advised me on my make-up and that afternoon, under her expert guidance, I crossed over the line from being a sometimes quite pretty, often not, ungainly and unsure young girl to a grown up woman, with a style that was all her own.

I began to be told I looked Spanish. Whether that was caused by my new hairdo— black curls and pale face—and liberal use of eye make-up, which was still unusual in those days, among respectable women at least. Which I was at that stage. Or perhaps as I grew older and the contours of my face became more defined, I actually did resemble my father.

Spain was very much in the news now. The Civil War galvanised popular attention. The heroic altruism of the International Brigade and the desperate plight of the Spanish Republicans began to play on our consciences. The fight against Fascism was taking shape as the moral crusade of our generation. Yolanda, with her knowledge of Italian Fascism, took sides early. She took up the Republican cause in Spain with all the passion and engagement that was in her nature. She went regularly to meetings, raised money for widows and orphans, and moved inexorably towards a socialist ideology.

Back at the Waldorf, we knew our place. Pandering shamelessly to the pampered few. With a new development that amused Mother. Occasionally, when the numbers were down, I was press ganged into participating in the Tango Teas which were held every afternoon in the Palm Court. It didn't bother me. In fact, I liked it; it provided a fascinating view of how the other half lived and was a welcome relief from the book keeping. The Palm Court was so beautiful, with its glass roof and balustrade, it took my breath away. It was the perfect setting for leisured elegance, a world of opera hats and immense private wealth, a way of life on which the sun was already setting.

It was probably because I wore my black suit most days and my earrings always. I was instructed to sit at a table and told firmly not to smile. So wearing black, earrings, black and looking po-faced was Spanish! Usually Freddy, who didn't look Spanish at all, was dragooned into being my partner. They must have been desperate. Still, as Yolanda said, a bit miffed because no-one had asked her, look on the bright side, it could have been a lot worse. You could have been tricked up with a rose in your teeth and a pair of castanets. She had a point.

The dancing was a bit of a shambles. Freddy's and my idea of the tango was very sketchy. Although we'd seen all the Rudolf Valentino films, we couldn't actually tango.

So we watched those who could (mercifully very few!) and bumped about trying to copy them. It was more of a frantic scramble than a dramatic *paso doble*. And we giggled a lot as we capered around the dance floor, making mincemeat of each other's feet, but nobody seemed to mind. They were just having fun anyway.

Chapter Seven

As the Thirties went on Yolanda, to her family's disquiet, became increasingly left-wing. She was outraged when the Labour Party annual conference adopted a policy of neutrality towards Spain as Franco, armed to the teeth by Hitler and Mussolini, marched on Madrid. She became distraught at what Mussolini was doing in her beloved Italy, becoming the friend and champion of those lucky few Italian dissidents, who had managed to make it to exile in London.

The focal point of all anti-Fascist feeling in London was Recchioni's wonderful food store in Old Compton Street. King Bomba, it was called. Recchioni was an old family friend and business associate of the Barronis. Papa B was one of his major suppliers, importing the wines, cheeses, salamis and superb olive oil from Lucca that had made them both rich and respected.

Recchioni hated Mussolini, so much so that he had even

funded two assassination attempts in the 1920s. When he died, his son took up the mantel and the shop became a meeting place and refuge for all Italian left-wingers. Vernon Recchioni was a great friend of Yolanda's. He was one of the first to see the significance of the Spanish Civil War and together they published the first weekly newspaper devoted to its coverage.

However, Yolanda's views caused ructions within the Barroni family. Ructions which, as ever, erupted at the dinner table. Papa had sympathised with his old partner, prophesising darkly that Mussolini would do Italy no good in the long run, but he would or could not take action against his fellow Italians, fearing perhaps for his business and Yolanda castigated him for "sitting on the fence."

She quarrelled openly with her younger brother, Carlo. Her older brother, Vittorio, was too busy helping Papa with the business, which was now far too big for one man to run. He went to and fro to Italy, recounting all that he had seen and clearly shocked by a lot of it, but, like Papa, he refused to become politically involved.

Carlo backed the Fascists. He thought they were entirely a good thing and would make Italy great again. Carlo was in some respects the odd one out in the Barroni family. He was short and fair, which made him look as if he did not quite belong. But what he lacked in stature, he made up in fervour. He was a true Barroni in that respect. Meal times became battle grounds, and no amount of placating or cajoling from the rest of us could prevent it.

"Mussolini may not be a great leader," he conceded at one of them, holding out a rare olive branch. His sister snorted. "But he will make Italy great." A whole orchestra of protest from a dismissive sniff from Papa, an operatic "No" from Mama to a howl of derision from Yolanda, greeted that remark. Vittorio looked at me and raised his eyes to heaven. I think he had been hoping against hope for a quiet family dinner.

"Carlo," you could understand his crossness as Yolanda now spoke to him softly, silkily, her tone caressing his wounded ego, while her words went straight for the jugular, "Caro, for once in your life, think. You must have a brain... somewhere," and she struck her forehead forcefully with the flat of her hand.

Carlo was beside himself. He started to stammer, "All I want... is... is..." She raised her eyebrows in query, with insulting politeness, "is for Italy to be great again. Don't you?" He made a final effort. "What kind of Italian are you?"

It wasn't fair. He hadn't a hope.

"A good one, darling. Who wants us to live up to the glories of our tradition. The home of Michelangelo and Mazzini—not the jackboot and the thug."

Choking with rage, Carlo banged his wine glass down on the table, sending a shower of blood red drops all over Mama's pristine lace tablecloth. She groaned, but before she could open her mouth, the battle went on.

"You're just a dreamer, Yolanda. A silly little girl with

big ideas. But you dream only of the past. We dream of the future."

Yolanda leaned in for the kill. "Your dream, Carlo, will become Italy's nightmare."

Game, set and match. Carlo glared at her, incandescent with rage, but with all his arguments exhausted. He never won any of these run-ins with his sister. Not any I ever saw, anyway.

Mama and Papa sighed. "Will they ever agree about anything?" Mama asked wearily as she began to collect the plates.

"No, cara, I don't think so," Papa replied, "We have brought Cain and Abel into the world."

Mama looked miserable as she left the room, but Papa was oddly undismayed. In fact, I thought he was secretly rather proud of his quarrelling off-spring, poles apart but articulate and informed.

Yolanda sat silently, defiant but shaken. These encounters always left her rather bereft, loathing as she did everything that Carlo believed in, but loving him just the same. She knew these were not like their past rows, bloody but soon forgotten. She said nothing, but her eyes were glittery with tears. I didn't know what to say. Papa smiled at me, "Don't look so worried, bambina. You know what they're like." I did, too.

While the spread of Fascism in Europe troubled us, the Spanish Civil War was the conflict that focused our attention. It preoccupied us; somewhere we knew that within its bitter struggle were the seeds of the war that would be ours. We dreaded even the thought of it. All of us had been brought up with the human damage of that first conflict all around us, and we tried hard to bury our heads in the sand, but somewhere we knew. Spain showed us that the battle that was coming would be decided in cities and streets with bombs and slaughtered civilians. There would be no battle honours for those burnt to death in their homes. The Spanish Civil War was our awakening—the anvil on which we forged the beliefs many of us would die for.

I was surprised how much I cared. I tried at first to shrug it off—what had Spain ever brought me but pain? But Yolanda wasn't having any of it—slowly but doggedly she refused to let me deceive myself, insisting I open my eyes, read the papers, think about what was happening in Spain, Italy and Germany. The threat of world Fascism was growing at a rate no-one could ignore, but here, in London, the police often turned a blind eye to Fascist violence. Prominent left-wingers and anarchists were beaten up and their premises broken into and vandalised. Many feared for their lives. Bearing in mind what was going on in Italy and Germany, it was a credible fear. Vero Recchioni, after being threatened by gunmen on more than one occasion, changed his name to Vernon Richards, hoping this anglicised identity would make him a less obvious target. But what finally brought it home to me, literally, was the sight of our Grenadier guards carrying the swastika draped coffin of the German Ambassador down the Mall, while Mosley's Blackshirts lined the route giving the Fascist salute.

After that, I began accompanying Yolanda to meetings, not just at Bomba's, but all over London, often in cold, dusty church halls where the debates were long and impassioned. It was a world away from the Waldorf.

At first, I felt horribly out of place. They all seemed so daunting. Many of them—men and women—were dressed like tramps, but they had much more than a few fancy clothes. They were bright and well-informed. Their minds and arguments had been honed in the debating halls of ancient universities. They were frighteningly well-read. Suddenly, I felt like a painted doll. The kind you cut out and stick on cardboard. I looked all right, but I had no substance. There was nothing to me; I felt shallow and stupid. While I had been fannying around, thinking I was so daring for earning a decent wage and getting my hair permed, they were engaging in the great issues of the day, trying to do something that mattered, not just hiding in an office between canyons of paper.

I often felt I was the only person at these gatherings who did not have a point of view. So I didn't speak because I didn't dare to. I would just clutch my glass of battery acid, as Yolanda called the wine, and listen.

At one of these meetings that took place in a private flat in Judd Street, I noticed a slim, dark man of about thirty-five sitting silently on the periphery. Like me, he listened intently but contributed nothing to the debate. Until another man opened it all out. He took the argument neatly away from the Spanish particular and launched into a tirade against the "great powers"—Britain, France and America—who prided themselves on being 'bastions of freedom', whilst ruthlessly repressing any spark of it in their colonies. At this the silent dark man came to life. He was from India, he informed the group, and an active member of the India League. He wanted freedom for India and he wanted it now. He felt that India should not passively wait for her current masters to dole out liberty in dribs and drabs; she had an intrinsic right to self-determination and should assume her place in the world as a free nation, not dependent on the by your leave of any other. Suddenly the room fell silent and I felt as if he were talking to me alone. I stood up. I had something to say. I knew about this. For the first time I spoke up. I said it was no use touting for freedom for the West alone, that freedom was either the birthright of all people in all places or it was just a fanciful notion, endlessly chewed over by those who had it but would not grant it to those who did not. It was a bit muddled politically speaking, and I don't know how I dared, but as far as India was concerned, I knew my stuff. All those hours reading in the library had paid off. I spoke of Ghandi and the Salt March, the Amritsar Massacre, the imprisonment of both Ghandi and Nehru and the historical legacy of the Mutiny. I could, and did, quote facts, figures and dates.

Then I noticed that everyone in the room was listening to me and I ground shakily to a halt, appalled at my outburst. I stopped abruptly in mid-sentence and sat down. The hubbub built up again around me. I stared down at my shoes, watching my legs shake. Adrenalin or fear, I wondered. Then I heard a voice. The dark man was standing in front of me.

"Well done! Well spoken. You have parted the waves for us here." He pointed to the room at large where heated discussion was taking place. He had an accent, but it was more of a lilt and very attractive. He smiled at me. Then a girl in a blue jumper piped up.

"I think you're completely wrong. India is a quite different case. We have built roads and railways..."

"Yes, you have. In order to move your troops in and our goods out. You have robbed us blind since the days of the East India Company."

She began to protest but he silenced her. "In any case the Grand Trunk Road and a few railways are not much of a swap for our freedom. We didn't ask you for any of this. It has benefited us very little, if at all."

I could have cheered. The group murmured its assent and she turned away, flushed with embarrassment. I liked this man. He winked at me and, as I smiled back, I felt as if we were the only two people in the room. In a moment the others ceased to have any significance to me. As the voices around us rose and fell, he said,

"Get your coat. Let's get out of here."

I did so without a second's hesitation.

I'm afraid I didn't give a thought to Yolanda or her friends. Rikh told me he was always known by his surname as his first name was a multi-syllable Rajput name—Viswanath—which was a "bit of a mouthful for most Brits." Indeed. Another bond. He took me to a pub nearby where we drank and talked and then to a modest restaurant where I remember nothing of the meal we ate, but our conversation that night has remained with me to this day. He was clever and astute and he didn't do small talk. He told me he was from Bangalore, an Indian city which had become a sort of Dorking.

"It's such arrogance, don't you see? Building rows and rows of quaint cottages in Karnataka?" I did. He went on.

"I'm probably a fool," (even then I knew he didn't think that for a second), "but like Gandhiji and Nehru I dream of a better world. Where all men are equal and the only things that divide us are the scope of our dreams, never the colour of our skins."

I thought he was wonderful.

"After all, like Shylock, we all suffer pain and feel joy." He looked down and ran his hand over his hair. Then he looked up and it seemed to me that his dark eyes were full of light.

"And we are all mortal. All men are born to die. But what we do in between is what makes us different. We can change the world. It won't be easy, but it can be done."

He reached across the table and took my hand. I felt that

he had taken what I had always felt, an inchoate set of ideas and made them concrete, realisable.

We talked for hours, mulling over everything and nothing until we were the last ones left in the restaurant, and the weary waiters, having cleared and wiped all the other tables, began to stack the chairs. When we saw them doing this we were aghast at the realisation of how long we had been there. Time had not just flown by, it had ceased to exist.

At one point he had asked me, "What made you so interested in India?"

It was a good question. "I don't really know."

Could I tell him that its profusion and diversity made it the opposite of everything I had ever known? That the conventions of the world I knew suffocated me and I longed to be free of them? To be somewhere, anywhere, where none of it mattered. I decided not. Instead, I hedged my bets.

"Why does anyone ever like anything or indeed anyone? What draws us to one thing and not another?"

I was thinking aloud really. I wondered if I sounded silly. But he smiled broadly at me.

"How interesting. Yes. I suppose all liking is a random instinct, a gathering together in the dark."

We left the restaurant. He walked me home through the damp London night and we talked some more. At one point we fell silent and just held hands. When he left me, politely and formally at my front door, I knew my life had changed forever.

He was by no means the best-looking man I had been out with, nor even the most intelligent, although he was both of those things; what he was for me was the most real. Our conversation reached a breadth and depth I had known with no one else. In the following days, all other interchanges seemed meaningless. A waste of time. Silly sounds to fill the silence while I waited, in limbo, for him to contact me.

He did. He wrote me a note saying that he had not been able to stop thinking about the things we had said and would I like to meet him again? He mentioned he would be attending a meeting of the India League in two days' time and perhaps I would be interested to attend as his guest? He didn't really have to ask.

I joined the India League as a full member that night and a few weeks later, Rikh and I became lovers. Through him and with him, I became part of a world of ideas. My axis changed, the froth and splendour of the Waldorf seemed like a dream, waking hours I walked through by necessity not choice. The world of scruffy student bedsits, dusty second-hand bookshops and cheap cafés became mine because it was his. And London, my home town, shifted like a kaleidoscope, as it had before with the Barronis, showing me a face so different it could have been another country, but one that had somehow managed to keep the stones and framework of my home. It was a glorious time.

Mother complained that I was never at home and she was right. I left the house at eight am and was rarely home before one or two. She lectured me about tiredness and burning the candle at both ends. I took no notice. She became increasingly anxious and was often awake when I returned home, flushed with love, intoxicated with youth and wine, walking on air. She tried to warn me—emphasizing our age difference, telling me not to "surrender too easily" as she had done, to wait and see if Rikh would prove to be 'the one', if it would stand the test of time. She might as well have tried to hold back Niagara; I was in love and it was a titanic force. Her cautious counsel didn't stand a chance.

Yolanda wasn't thrilled either. She didn't really like Rikh, "a dry stick" she called him. He was too calm and measured for her, she too impassioned and mercurial for him. They had a kind of mutual regard, a sort of wary respect for each other, but they were always uneasy in each other's company. She took me out to lunch again at the ABC, always Yolanda's place of choice for warnings and over beans on toast gave me a thorough grilling along Mother's lines.

When I told her she was too late, I loved him and, in any case, we were already lovers, she sighed operatically, ran her hands through her hair in a gesture of complete hopelessness and took me that afternoon after work to a funny old lady in Cricklewood with piercing blue eyes, who fitted me with a Dutch cap and showed me how to use it. She had been a nurse in the First World War, at the field hospital in Etaples she said, and there she had seen enough unwanted pregnancies to last her a lifetime. Men have to be half-dead, broken in mind and body, she said, before they give up on sex. I got a bit huffy at that. There was nothing broken about my lover, I announced proudly. "All the more reason for you to be careful, then, isn't there?" she replied brusquely, putting the cap into a little box and snapping the lid shut. There was no answer to that. So I took her advice and paid her ten shillings for the cap and the Volpar gel to put on it.

It all upset me rather. Rikh asked me what was wrong when I met him afterwards, a little late, because the bus from Cricklewood had taken ages. I told him the whole story, a little tearful by now. He put his arm round me and sighed.

"She could have trusted me to be careful."

"Who?"

"Yolanda. Doesn't like me much, does she?"

I tried to explain that I didn't think it was a question of that, rather that she was trying to protect me.

"I know. But I thought that was my job."

He brushed my hair off my forehead.

"Poor little baby. We should have dealt with this together." I tried to explain.

"My fault. Not yours. In any case," he reached for his beer, "she's jealous."

"Yolanda? You're crazy! Men go nuts about her."

"She's not jealous of you, silly. She's jealous of me." I thought that unlikely.

"Or rather she is jealous of us. Yolanda can have anyone, but she has no one, does she?"

She hadn't actually. I had never thought of it like that before. She was always in a crowd, the centre and star of it, she had the admiration and envy of many, but never the adoration of one was how he put it. The trouble with Rikh was, he was invariably right. I shrugged it off. No-one else really mattered to me at that time. I loved Yolanda, as I did my mother, but they seemed suddenly pale, shadows eclipsed by the noon-time glare of my love.

And we were serious, Rikh and I. We had a purpose. A mission. India.

Chapter Eight

We worked tirelessly for the India League. As an MA student in Advanced Aeronautics at Imperial College, Rikh had more time than I did, but we both spent most of our free time at the League offices. They were situated in a tall, narrow building in the Strand—three large dusty rooms on the first floor overlooking the Thames. It was a shabby, ramshackle place, almost Dickensian in character with torn lino on the floor, peeling paint on the windows and dust an inch thick everywhere. We, the members, were far too important and high minded to clean. I tried to, once, but gave up after a few minutes, when the swirling dust made everyone cough and they all complained that I was interrupting the serious nature of the work.

So instead I took minutes and typed reports and agendas for the committee meetings we attended. I roneo'd hundreds of copies, not always successfully, there was always some part of the page where the ink did not come through. I addressed envelopes by the thousand: there was a big nationwide drive on then to raise awareness in the provinces. Well, more in the industrial heartland where the working class felt badly about their own conditions and could empathise with the down-trodden colonies.

We were a motley crew in the India League in those years, utterly disparate in background, class and education. There were socialists and intellectuals, old Etonians and grammar school boys, communists, anarchists and wealthy Indians called to the Bar in London. We all pitched in together and worked for a better world. I typed and filed and addressed and made Krishna Menon, the mastermind behind it all, hundreds of cups of tea (he drank about 34 cups a day!) but most of all, I made friends. I liked them a lot. They were all intelligent and driven, but never pompous. We had a very serious aim—the downfall of Empire—but we were mostly young and we had great fun plotting it.

Krishna Menon was a man of many and varied achievements, a brilliant barrister, co-founding editor of Penguin Books, instigator of the Travelling Library. He was, as Lord Listowell said later—a vitriolic, impatient and intolerant man, who suffered mere mortals not a lot and fools not at all, but he could also be sensitive and considerate, and was at his best "a great teacher and a great man." He dominated our group entirely; his word was law and he was the driving force behind all our activities. He had been dubbed "a serious menace" by British security (a title he was rather proud of) and had been under police surveillance since 1929. His mail was often intercepted and he was sometimes followed. It didn't bother him at all. He maintained a lofty disdain for his adversaries in the British Establishment that rubbed off to some degree on all of us.

Rikh and I grew closer and closer until we came to feel all time spent apart was wasted. We only parted to sleep and not always then. Mother hated it when I started spending the night in his digs. She didn't approve and was fearful for me. I told her about the cap, hoping to allay her fears, but I only succeeded in shocking her. Her generation didn't even talk about birth control, let alone practise it. Her anxiety was aggravated by the fact that she, like Yolanda, didn't warm to Rikh. The few times I brought him home resulted in awkward silences. The tension made them both revert to type horribly. She took refuge in dour Scots disapproval, pursing her lips so that the lines around her mouth stood out in the way I knew and hated; and he hid behind a kind of silky Indian diffidence that felt patronising to me and looked like arrogance to her.

At first I even wondered if she didn't like him because he was Indian. Remarks had been made at work after he had met me at the staff door, sniggering asides, half heard, hostile stares and comments about "the tar brush" were made. I couldn't have cared less. And I silenced Mother forever with a comment about how her relatives had clearly not approved of her taking up with a 'Dago', so who was she to disapprove of me? She allowed herself to look really hurt, then turned away, saying softly that she had always hoped my path in life would be an easier one than hers had been. After that she said no more. But she feared for me and this created a chasm between us. I stayed out more after that, often staying overnight in Rikh's rooms in Marchmont Street (so much nearer to work, I told her) or meeting for a snatched breakfast in the ABC on the days when I did not.

In the end, I barely lived at home at all.

It was a total involvement. My love affair with India, if you like, both in the person of Rikh and in the political arena of the League, consumed my waking hours and left very little room for anything else.

I still saw Yolanda at work every day, but our joint socialising and family times ceased. I didn't love her any less, I just didn't need her patronage anymore. I don't know if that bothered her. She never mentioned it, but I had always been her devoted acolyte and my defection may have made her feel a bit vulnerable, even lonely. I don't know. She never said.

Life had begun to take us in opposing directions. Although we were now both engaged politically—her sphere was all about ideology and the general. Her left-wing bias and hatred of European fascism was driving her towards world communism whereas my involvement was highly particular. My struggle had a different focus:

freedom for me was all about one place and it wore a very human face. Rikh's.

All this impacted on our friendship. I had very little free time now, and she none at all it seemed. She lived in and for the meetings: groups of people suited her very well, she was born to command them. Whereas even my attendance at the League meetings, which I attended religiously, were only really preludes to a greater involvement, a deeper closeness with Rikh. I was so much in love. We were always together now and it had an inevitability about it. It was not that I loved her less, it was just that I loved him more.

I moved in with Rikh on a Saturday afternoon in July. It was warm and sunny, the white billowing clouds scudding joyously across a clear blue sky, and my whole world seemed to be opening up. Rikh and I carried my few possessions out of the house and loaded them into an old Ford that belonged to a friend of his and was borrowed for the occasion. It felt very grown-up and swish. There wasn't much—a battered suitcase, which had belonged to Cornelius, the only person in our orbit who had ever owned such a thing, held together by a belt, a few books, Mrs Lomasney's little china vase with violets painted on it—it was always on her dressing table and she had given it to me because I loved it. There was very little else. We drank tea and ate the cake my mother had baked, almost in silence. The enormity of what I was doing beginning to sink in.

Then I hugged her goodbye, refusing to register the naked grief on her face, and told her all the lies neither of us believed. How I would see her often, come home all the time, how we could meet in town, go shopping etc. I babbled on, wanting to comfort but meaning none of it. We both knew what this meant. She was being banished to the sidelines of my life, and I had only ever been the centre of hers. My senseless chatter dried up and we clung to each other as if drowning. Then she pulled away and fixed me with what I had always called "her Scottish stare".

"We will meet once a week. Thursday evenings, six o'clock sharp in the Ladies Bar of the Cumberland Hotel. Every week, Juanita, you will be there and so will I."

We were too. She was always first, waiting for me, two small schooners of sweet sherry in front of her. Hair smoothed back, shoes polished. Without fail. The guy-rope of my life.

Soon after we left her that day, Rikh stopped the car. I wondered if there was something wrong with it. Then he said, "You mustn't be afraid of leaving her. I will look after you, you know."

I stared at him blankly. Had he not noticed how eager I was to leave, to embrace adult life with him?

He leaned across and kissed me.

"What a child you are, darling," he said softly. Then he started the car and drove on, leaving me somewhat bemused. How had he failed to see that I was totally preoccupied with my new life? A home of my own. A man of my own. The India League. Even the Waldorf. No one was more impressed by it all than me.

While Rikh and I settled in together, learning the realities of a shared life in two small rooms, with a cupboard kitchen and a shared bathroom, things were hotting up in the political arena. A series of strikes and riots had erupted in Bombay and were put down with unprecedented harshness. The rioters were flogged and a wave of arrests of political activists swept through the sub-continent.

As a result, to our joy, when elections were held in nine of the eleven provinces in British India (Princely India did not hold elections), Congress scored a massive victory. In London, we held a celebration party, spilling out onto the pavement in the cold wet dawn, laughing and hugging each other, convinced that the worst was over and freedom and independence were only just around the corner. Alas.

In India Congress was almost immediately in deadlock with the Viceroy, Lord Linlithgow, who refused to rule out the use of emergency powers. As ever, we played naively by the rules of democracy while the Empire ploughed on, riding roughshod over the principles it claimed to cherish.

In Europe, if anything, the situation was worse. Yolanda became totally preoccupied with trying to get dissidents out of Italy. Elsewhere Hitler was on the march. The Anschluss was greeted with hysterical joy by the Austrians, then came Munich, both the euphoria of false hope and the dawning grim awareness. Yolanda said we in the League should wake up, that there was a far greater struggle looming that would sweep away all old Empires and would have to be won if anything we held dear was to survive. Slowly, still encased in my bubble, I began to open my eyes and look nearer home. The battle lines were being drawn.

The only indication Krishna ever gave that he trusted my opinion came out of the blue that autumn. It was a cold, blustery afternoon in late October, a Saturday when the rough wind shook the few remaining leaves from the skeleton trees and the damp air promised winter. We had worked hard at the League offices all morning—one of my rare Saturdays off from work—and Rikh and I had rewarded ourselves with a long lunch at the Lyons Corner House in the Strand. Their cabinet pudding was the Saturday special and it was a great favourite of ours. We returned late, replete and a bit guilty, to find the office empty. Except for Krishna, who was sitting at his desk in the inner sanctum, glaring out into the main office with the air of a disgruntled eagle.

"Where is everybody?" I asked breezily, deciding that levity was the way to defuse this particular bout of ill humour. It worked sometimes. There was an awkward silence as Rikh took his coat off.

"I sent them home." Krishna was such an autocrat. We waited in frozen silence for the next edict.

"I've had word that we are about to be paid a visit from the gentlemen of the Metropolitan Police."

The penny didn't take long to drop. "Oh God, my lists!" I had spent days compiling a full set of lists of all our members' names and addresses, and perhaps more importantly, details of all our sponsors, together with the size and dates of their donations.

"Precisely, Juanita." Then he looked me carefully up and down. I couldn't imagine why now. He never had before. Frankly, I thought his timing a bit off.

"You'll do." He reached down and handed me a shabby old briefcase.

"Now take it and get lost." Rikh looked horrified. He began to demur.

"No, not you. Her." Rikh started to stutter something about me being very vulnerable alone.

"Don't be such a fool. Who's going to suspect her? She's white, British and oh so respectable. Looking, anyway."

I wasn't sure I liked that.

"No, she's perfect. Fashion mad office girl out shopping on a Saturday afternoon. Ten a penny. No one'll give her a second glance."

I was a bit insulted by that, but I could see his point. I had dressed smartly for our Saturday lunch. Black costume, neat little blouse, pearl earrings, even gloves because it was cold and, for once in my life, a hat. Unusually for that era, I didn't often wear a hat. I didn't like them, but I had made an exception for this one. It was a black felt matador's hat, worn at a dashing angle, with a gold braid strap under the chin. It had cost me a small fortune. It all sounds a bit silly now, but at the time I thought it was the last word in chic.

"Okay. I'll do it." I was stepping up to the plate there all right, but I was scared. It was desperately illegal after all. And I would be alone. I wasn't given the chance to prevaricate.

"Good girl. Now scram! Get on a bus or something and don't come back for at least four hours. When you do, look around carefully, and if you see the hint of a copper or anything a bit fishy, vanish. But don't go home. Go shopping. Wait another few hours and then come and find me in The Wellington. I'll be waiting for you there."

I must have looked a bit dumb-founded because he said, "Got it?"

I had and not a moment too soon because as I was walking downstairs as sedately as I could with my heart beating so hard I could hear it in my ears, four burly policemen burst in and thundered past me. Krishna was right. They didn't give me a second glance. Except for one. "Sorry, Miss," he panted as he shoved me out of the way.

I was shaking as I walked to the bus stop. I spent the rest of the afternoon and early evening on top of a number 13 bus, riding round London in the rain. From the Strand all the way out to Golders Green and back again. An old briefcase innocuously on my lap, containing the contact details of those the Metropolitan Police had decided posed a "serious threat" to the security of the realm.

From then on, the pressure on us was ramped up. Police

surveillance was increased, sometimes in an absurdly heavy-handed fashion. Raids were carried out on the Rawalpindi barrister who sold sweets to other Indians living in London and the little book shop in Great Russell Street, run by a Bengali, both mild and inoffensive men. Hardly the Trotskys of our movement. Krishna, who arguably was, was now followed round the clock by a series of rather surly detectives. One of whom he used to greet cheerily every morning. He even offered him the shelter of his umbrella on one occasion. He had the cheek of the devil, Krishna. He had utter contempt for his enemies, but he wasn't averse to using charm if all else failed. He crowed with delight at the discomfiture of his police detail, divining early that the British were not loath to indulge in political skulduggery, but "awful reluctant to be found out." We often roared with laughter at his tales of the woefully dumb police who simply couldn't keep up with him. To be fair, not many could. All of us in the League were blasted into the sidelines by the brilliance of his mind and the sheer force of his personality. He towered above his contemporaries, able to demolish any rival for the limelight with his caressing, sarcastic wit and a silky ease that made it even more insulting. There was only ever one star turn in the India League. No one else stood a chance.

But as time wore on and the police pressure increased, the accuracy of their information made it obvious to us that we had an informer in our midst. It was a chilling thought. As a result, an inner committee of the most trustworthy was formed, of which Rikh and I were a part, and the decision was taken to encode all our most secret documents and records, principal among which were my lists of members and sponsors.

Even Rikh's mail was tampered with now. It was being made clear to us that politics was not a game and that advocating the end of Empire and home rule for India was an act of sedition.

The codes worried me. It seemed to me that an averagely bright child could crack them. However, the rest of the committee felt that the Metropolitan Police could not. I plucked up my courage and went to see Krishna. I told him I thought the codes were far too simple and the assumption that all policemen were morons was foolhardy. He screwed his eyes up against the smoke from his everlasting cigarette; his cubby hole of an office was so full of smoke that I longed to throw open the window, but he would never allow it. So I coughed and spluttered and tried to make my point. He dismissed me with a look of disdain that would have done Queen Mary proud. Waving me aside like the insignificant minnow that I was he said,

"When I require advice on how to run a subversive movement I will ask for it. Until then may I request that you focus your attention on the agenda for this evening's meeting, so that the unfortunates souls attending will have some idea of why they are here."

That was it. Lady Bracknell in a lounge suit. You couldn't argue with him. I went back to my menial duties.

But I did notice that several days later the main code had been changed and was now much more impenetrable. But not enough. Not to my eyes anyway.

Chapter Nine

I soon learned one thing about life with Rikh. Whilst fervently advocating freedom for the many, he wouldn't countenance it for the few; and for those closest to him not at all. As I lived with him and shared his life in almost every aspect I discovered that, on a domestic level at least, he was alarmingly autocratic. It seemed to me a very double standard. At first I put it down to his superior age and intellect, then as I learned more about him, I thought it was rather due to his extremely privileged background. Although only the junior branch (second son of second son), it was nonetheless an aristocratic and wealthy family and he had clearly been used to having what he wanted when he wanted it. Here in London, this was carried over as his intelligence and quick wit gave him a dominance his status as a colonial student didn't really merit. And he wasn't always like that. He could be kind and thoughtful when he wanted to. So I put his rather peremptory arrogance down to a tone of voice rather than a frame of mind and didn't take much notice.

Until one evening about two months after we started to live together, I planned an ambitious meal. Until then we had made do with café meals, Joe Lyons was always a favourite; Rikh didn't seem to mind, as an avid people watcher, he liked going out as much as I did. And on the rare occasion when we were too tired to go out and "forage" as he called it, we had snacky food of the egg and bacon on a tray variety at home. But I decided I should try for something better at least sometimes and this time I went for broke.

Tomato soup, chicken in a mustard sauce (he liked food with a tang and some colour to it, "bland mush" as he called it, revolted him) and a beautiful rhubarb tart. I had collected the tart from Mother over our usual sherry at the Cumberland. That at least was perfect. We had had a very pleasant time, she and I, talking, laughing over some trivial incident at work, and so I was a bit late getting home. As soon as I got back I rolled up my sleeves, put the pinny on and set to work. By the time Rikh got home about an hour later I was hot and bothered, but prepared to be flushed with triumph.

He surveyed the scene of my labours, I hadn't had time yet to clear up, smiled encouragingly and graciously poured out two large glasses of wine. We drank them and then I got ready to serve.

The soup, perhaps not cooked for long enough, was

very thin and oddly tasteless, more like a kind of brightly coloured hot water. We sipped at it and crumbled our bread rolls, brought at lunchtime from the ABC, so they were all right, and after a few polite mouthfuls, agreed that soup wasn't really "our thing." So I threw most of it away and dished up the main course. It was a catastrophe. The Belling stove was very old and woefully underpowered. It took ages just to heat up. So the chicken covered in its lovely bright yellow mustard sauce was raw, almost blue inside, the peas were like tiny emerald rocks and the new potatoes were so hard you couldn't pin them down with a fork, when we tried they rolled smartly across the plate and bounced onto the floor like little cannonballs.

"Nita," Rikh had christened me that, Juanita was too much of a mouthful even for him, "nothing on this plate is edible." He sounded so incredulous I had to resist a sudden urge to laugh. You had to laugh really. It was all so awful.

I suppressed it, but not quickly enough. He had seen me.

"It's not funny." And he banged his fist on the table and the potatoes and peas jumped about on the plates. I laughed out loud at that. I couldn't help it. It was either that or cry.

"Well, the pud's okay. Mother made that." For some reason, maybe the wine? I found that even funnier. The expression on his face was so ill-tempered, so overwhelmingly disapproving, I couldn't help it. The Rikh

I knew had disappeared. Suddenly I was having dinner with Mr Barrett of Wimpole Street.

"I don't want pudding!" He was really angry. "I want a meal! I'm not asking for the earth, but I do want something I can eat at the end of a very long day!" What was he talking about? He was a student for God's sake. My working hours were far longer than his. He banged the table again and I could feel my laughter flowing away like water down a drain.

"Rikh, I am sorry. I really tried. I just couldn't get the Belling thing right. The settings are all wrong." I hoped reason would placate him. He was a man who believed in reason after all. But he just glared at me and swept his plate off the table onto the floor where it smashed.

"I'm going out. And if you can't even put together a simple meal I will be going out a lot more often."

He flounced out of the room like a child having a tantrum, stamping through his scattered food and broken plate. Then he left, slamming the front door behind him.

I cleared up the mess, sweeping the meal I had tried so hard with into the bin, and then I cried, wondering how I had managed to come full circle. It was like being back with Cornelius. Rikh had never been like this before. But I was back again, living with a domestic tyrant. I wondered if I had failed to pick up the warning signs; I racked my brains, but I couldn't think of any. The whole storm seemed to have come out of a clear sky. Just like before. Only the last time around I hadn't been alone; last time

I had had Mother. By the time I had finished crying and clearing up, I was really hungry. So I cut myself a piece of pie and ate it. It was very good, but it only made me wish I was back with her. I washed up my plate and went to bed early. When Rikh got back some hours later, I pretended I was asleep.

The next morning I made tea in silence. We drank it without looking at each other, then Rikh said, "I'm sorry." He didn't sound it. I turned away. He got up and took me in his arms, brushing my hair off my face. "Look we'll have to sort it out, little baby, or we'll starve. I'll get back early tonight and, if necessary, we'll do it together."

I nodded in agreement, but I didn't want to. He was all right now, the next morning they always are. But I was not. He bustled on, getting his jacket, putting his papers into his briefcase, oblivious to the fact that he had broken far more than a plate.

The incident passed without either resolution or understanding. We didn't talk about it. Normal life took over and we were carried along by the ordinary. Work for us both, meetings at the League, long evenings spent discussing life, books, politics, at restaurants over pasta and Chianti, trips to the theatre. Everything was to inform, evoke thought—now I think to provide us with an alibi. We sought to solve all problems but our own.

We used to go regularly to the theatre. But not the West End shows that so delighted the clientele of the Waldorf. Music and laughter, red plush and orchestra stalls were not for us. A favourite of ours was the Group Theatre which performed the avant-garde plays of the time—Eliot, Auden and Isherwood. Often in blank verse, they were experimental, so we felt that we were at the cutting edge of something, but we were never terribly sure what. Some were wonderful, but not many. "Worthy but not often enjoyable" was Rikh's verdict and, as ever, he was right. Still, we were diligent if nothing else and we travelled all over London to see these plays. Hampstead, Barnes and Notting Hill usually; we trundled across London on the bus, to watch and be informed, and then trundled back home, often in the rain. The venues for these plays were always dusty and often unheated, we sat on bare wooden benches, and I came to equate intellectual worth with physical discomfort. Perhaps it was a small price to pay for not having to spend an evening at home together. At least, that's how it seems to me now.

In time the meal problem solved itself. Rikh was not a monster, after all. Now I feel rather sorry for him. An older, far more mature man, he was fifteen years older than I was after all and used to a standard of living I had never enjoyed. He bravely took a paternalistic stance with a giddy, mixed up girl and tried to make the best of it. Overwhelmed by my own boldness, I never stopped to consider his. That the arc of his journey was far greater than mine. Blinded by my own pride in what I saw as my lack of prejudice and refusal to bow to the conventions of the time, I failed to even consider what his family would have made of me. Not much, I imagine. A dynastic marriage on his return to India was what they wanted for him: a young woman of spotless virtue, good family and wealth was what they had in mind. And what had he shackled himself with? A silly dependent child, playing at being Bohemian, and a bastard to boot. Not only not of good family, but of no family at all. Their worst nightmare.

The discrimination that I so boastfully rose above, he dealt with in reverse and in silence. His Indian friends must have asked him how he could ever be happy with me —a memsahib with no money or status. The worst of all worlds. An Empress with no clothes. He said nothing of this at the time, but he told me later. When it was too late. It worries me now what he went through alone as I passed through it all unable or unwilling to see. Blind to all but my own dilemma.

I did try to improve on the cooking though. Rikh had never let me contribute towards our expenses. He paid for everything with good grace, refusing to accept even the gift of an occasional meal out. For all his modern ideas, he was oddly old-fashioned in that respect. So I was now much richer than I had ever been, although I still gave Mother half my wages. She could not have managed without it.

I thought the least I could do was learn to cook a bit. Mother gave me some rudimentary lessons on Sunday mornings when Rikh slept in late, and although I never lived up to her skill, she got me to the stage that I could reliably produce four or five dishes, that were just about edible. Shepherd's pie, sausage and mash with onion gravy, liver and bacon, and grilled sole, I formed my limited repertoire. Puddings I either got from Mother on a Thursday or did without. I didn't think I could be trusted with them. And Rikh seemed happy enough. At least he was kind and encouraging, and did eat it all, though I did notice that he always liberally sprinkled his food with a chopped green or red chilli bought in Berwick Street market, so it can't have been that good.

Thankfully, what with the meetings and the theatre, we did eat out a lot. You could eat out reasonably well for not too much money in those days in cafés and small restaurants (mostly in Soho) friendly and welcoming places where the food was good and the wine was cheap. It was nothing grand and certainly neither of us were gourmets. We were far too earnest for that.

Yolanda tried to convert us by taking us to Bertorelli's, then the favourite haunt of actors, intellectuals and students from the nearby university. Her father was a family friend, if not distant cousin, of the owners, and we had many lovely meals there. Good Italian as Yolanda was she didn't see lofty principles and enjoyment of life as mutually exclusive. She enjoyed the good things in life with a gusto that I had long envied but still eluded me, however hard I tried to kid myself. I think it was the legacy of my Mother's Calvinism or the terrible price she had paid for her brief idyll with my father. Whatever it was, I had imbibed her fear of license to some extent. Although paradoxically, I secretly longed for an oceanic passion, an all-consuming love that would overcome everything. A love I was slowly beginning to realise I did not share with Rikh.

Meanwhile life at the Waldorf went on, utterly unaffected by the momentous events taking place outside its opulent cocoon. Munich came and went, Czechoslovakia was parcelled up and sold down the river, and all but the most blinkered of us now knew that war would come—it was only a question of when. But none of this was allowed to affect life at the Waldorf. There light and luxury reigned. The greatest drama, a misplaced booking or a fallen soufflé. It was another world, all right, but, to tell the truth, after the fervour of the League, not always an unwelcome one.

My working life had become a lot more pleasant. I had tackled any task the General Manager threw at me, and here Mother's work ethic and my solid education paid off. The GM began to consult me. He was not a bad man to work for. He liked to keep his God-like status in front of other hotel staff, but within the sanctum of his office, he was oddly democratic. At least, with Yolanda and me. But perhaps that was because he had the whole Italian community of London peering over his shoulder and scrutinising his every move! The Barroni tribe. They were a power to reckon with all right and I wouldn't have put it past them to keep a protective and highly partisan eye on us both. They regarded that as normal.

Anyway, hard work or nepotism, whatever the cause, I was promoted. I was no longer a lowly clerk of all work, but now went under the somewhat ambiguous title of Special Assistant to the General Manager, as opposed to the Senior Assistant which Yolanda was. Freddy didn't have a new title. He was still stuck with the old one. I also had quite a bit more money.

Special Assistant only seemed to mean that a huge range of miscellaneous tasks could be assigned to me—from in depth profit and loss analyses to checking that Gorringes still stocked the particular shade of kid gloves the Maharani of Jhalawar was partial too. She was a regular guest in the hotel. She came to London for shopping every year, but she rarely left her suite. I think she expected the shopping to come to her and mostly it did. With a bit of help from us.

Freddy was seriously miffed because I was promoted above him. It can't have been easy—sandwiched between Yolanda and me. Our long friendship and shared education meant we tackled things with the same method, using a sort of spoken shorthand he could not penetrate. He got left behind, frankly. He was very sniffy at first, no longer taking coffee and tea breaks with me or sitting with us in the canteen at lunchtime. The Tango teas got very awkward. One day he was so silent and sullen I couldn't stand it. The atmosphere between us was like a brick wall. I had to break it.

"I'm sorry, Freddy."

"What for?" He whirled me around none too gently, stepping over my feet as if they were something a dog had left behind on the pavement.

"Taking your promotion," I mumbled, not daring to look at his face.

"You haven't." I was so flustered I messed up the tango and trod heavily on his left foot. He glared at me.

"Anyway," he said as he steered me around at arms' length, "you only got it because you're a girl. We all know what the GM is for the ladies." I was pretty sure that wasn't true, but I smiled weakly and tried to placate him,

"I expect you're right." He looked sternly at me.

"Still running round with that nigger?" That did it. All sympathy snapped. I kicked him.

"What d'ya want to do that for?"

"Because he is a better man than you will ever be. In every way."

With that, I wrenched his arm round and changed direction. We nearly collided with an elderly couple who looked suitably alarmed. Freddy looked coldly at me.

"All your chums are Dagoes or Wogs. Couldn't you find anyone English?"

"No. And if they're all like you, what a blessing that is." I set my jaw and executed a pretty snappy *paso doble*. He had trouble keeping up. I am half-Spanish after all. I wrenched his arm and changed direction again. He stopped dead on the dance floor. We faced each other breathlessly, like fighting children.

"Gawd, I surrender! You're a dark horse. Normally butter wouldn't melt. Talk about the worm turning."

"Don't push your luck, Freddy." I tugged a stray lock of hair out of my eyes and walked off the dance floor.

"Crikey!" He was so phased he'd forgotten his elocution. He followed me.

"Female of the species and all that. How about a cuppa tea and a calm down?" I was too cross to reply.

"If that's not too English for you?"

I glared at him, but said nothing. I didn't want to have a slanging match in public. That would have got us both the sack. So we sat down and had tea and he told confessed to me that he was "sore" about the promotion because he was saving up to get married. He was engaged to Veronica in Housekeeping and they had their eye on a nice little flat in Ruislip. They had been saving for three years and he had hoped that the promotion would "put the cap on it." I felt bad then because with Rikh being so generous, I didn't need the extra money and Freddy clearly did.

The next day I told Yolanda about it.

"Too bad. He's an arse." She paused there and blew a perfect smoke ring. She was awfully good at that. Admiringly, I watched it disperse.

"He is also ideologically the enemy." That was just too silly.

"Freddy's not anyone's enemy. He's too limited for that."

That was greeted by one of her sudden barks of laughter.

"In his outlook, I mean."

She laughed even more. "Sure. And the rest." She looked fondly at me, like an amused parent.

"Well, I feel sorry for him."

"Ah. And you want me to help nasty little Freddy and his cretinous Veronica sail off into the sunset to wedded bliss in Ruislip."

I hadn't thought it through, but that was about the size of it. I nodded.

"With all his hatred of Dagoes—that's us by the way—and Wogs like your beloved Rikh intact?"

Put like that it didn't sound too good, but I still felt sorry for him. He had been humiliated after all and he had been so kind when I first started. I pointed this out.

She sighed.

"Only because he wanted to get into your knickers, child."

I trailed my spoon through the sugar bowl, watching the mountains of tiny grains rise and fall. I always did that when I was uneasy. She went on.

"So you want me to ask my father—Chief Wop—to find Freddy a well paid job he doesn't deserve? Is that it?"

"Um... more or less." Never any point beating around the bush with her. The mountains of sugar rose and fell.

She finished her cigarette in silence, then stubbed it out, grinding it viciously into the ashtray.

"You've got a nerve." She was smoking a lot these days. Senior Service. Terribly strong. Her fingers were becoming stained with nicotine. She shook her head and picked up the bill.

"It's a good job I love ya." And she walked briskly across the café to the cashier. I put the spoon down and my gloves on, smiling, knowing the deed was as good as done.

It was. The following week Freddy burst into my office, red faced and radiant.

"I've been offered a job! Out of the blue!" I looked up.

"S'marvellous! Pay's out of this world!" Yolanda had somewhat exceeded her brief, it seemed. Old Freddy was on cloud nine.

"Little hotel—family-run, near Regent's Park. I'll be the manager really." I doubted that.

"That's wonderful, Freddy."

"Isn't it? Chance of a lifetime. And Veronica and me..." He was so chuffed he couldn't go on. I stood up and put my hand out

"Congratulations. I'm really happy for both of you." He was so carried away he ignored my outstretched hand and hugged me. Which shocked the pair of us. But perhaps he had an inkling after all? We pulled apart, rigid with embarrassment.

"Er... No offence."

"None taken." I didn't know where to look.

"Might be best not to mention..." He was already halfway out of the door. "Veronica might not..."

"Mum's the word." He nodded his thanks and was off to spread the good news.

When I thanked Yolanda she gave me an evil grin.

"Don't thank me. He'll be working for Uncle Vittorio and his sons. If Old Freddy doesn't shape up they'll make his life hell. As only a Dago can."

"I thought Uncle Vittorio had been cast out forever?"

She shrugged, "You know the score. Family is forever. Anger... a little less. "

I grinned back. You had to love that girl.

But Freddy, like many others, never got the chance to realise his dream. Within a few short weeks, he was overtaken by events. Events that would tear apart our normal world and throw us round the globe, the flotsam and jetsam of war.

Chapter Ten

I never forgot the moment when I first saw him. It was a day like any other—dull, unmemorable except for this—I didn't know what it meant at the time, but I never forgot it.

He checked into the hotel on the following Monday. An ordinary Monday—late morning, nearly lunchtime—in the lull between the weekend guests' departure and the new week's intake. After the first flurry of activity there was always a pause, a hiatus when the hotel had a hushed, expectant air, waiting for the week to begin.

I was shocked when I first saw him. He walked briskly through the lobby and up to reception to check in. Freddy and I were having our coffee late and we were lingering over it, gossiping with Betty, who ran reception. She nearly dropped her cup at the sight of him and, following her gaze, I could see why.

Real beauty is rare. As rare as real ugliness. The sight of either is startling and rather unsettling. Most of us muddle through in a haze of the middle ground—"pretty or handsome, attractive, good-looking." He was none of these. If the rest of us were houses, he was a cathedral. It was a Westminster Abbey of a face. A place where flesh and bone met in complete harmony. The huge dark eyes, the high cheekbones, the soft, full mouth—there was no doubt about it—he was beautiful. I couldn't take my eyes off him.

He was tall, slim and very smart—from his perfectly cut Savile Row suit to the glassy finish on his hand-made shoes. The only points of colour were the deep sapphire silk of his tie and the paler blue of his turban. He was a Sikh. Freddy knew him of old, he said, "...been coming here for years. Ever since he went up to Oxford. Rich as Croesus. Never stays long. Only just the few days. Always on his way somewhere else. Takes the Astor suite."

Freddy mumbled this out of the side of his mouth. He always knew everything about all the guests. He was an inveterate gossip; keeping "his eyes open" as he put it, or his ears flapping as I did. He took over from poor old Betty, who seemed pole-axed. He pushed her aside, filled in the book then gave it to the man to sign. Then he handed him his key and rang for the porter, who came running, or as near to running as Old George could manage. He had been the Head Porter at the Waldorf for as long as anyone could remember and he came positively sprinting across from his desk, elbowing aside his bevy of bellhops.

He picked up the luggage and trundled off towards the lift, his lumbago, so often complained of, suddenly vanished. I turned to Freddy,

"What...?"

"George won't let anyone else go near him. Tips like money's going out of style. Pound notes sometimes. Son of a Prince. Gold coming out of his ears."

I stared after him until the lift doors closed. Although this man was Indian, he was about as unlike Rikh as it was possible to be.

The rest of the day passed in a sort of dream. Later that afternoon, after I had finished work I was in no hurry to go home because Rikh was away. He had gone to Hatfield for a week on a training secondment at De Havilland's and Yolanda had rushed off to one of her meetings, so I went to chat with Betty. She wasn't at reception so I hung around a bit, hoping to find someone to talk to. He passed me on his way to the bar, smiled and then turned round and came back.

"Hello. Do you work here?"

"Yes." Breathing had suddenly become difficult.

He smiled again. "I don't know if you'd mind? I'm at a bit of a loose end. Perhaps you would take pity and have a drink with me?"

The charm was very smooth. He was awfully sure of himself, a bit big-headed really, and I'm afraid I did nothing to make it less. I nodded, not daring to speak and then disgraced myself by doing a lively impersonation of

George, galloping after him across the foyer before anyone else could get their hands on him.

I sat down by the window and looked out, trying to recover some composure. He spoke to the barman and then sat down. An ice bucket appeared almost immediately—beads of moisture on its metal surface, a black bottle of champagne resting on its bed of ice, with two flute glasses and some caviar canapés.

"I hope you like this stuff?"

I nodded. He grinned "Can you actually speak? Because..."

I had to laugh at that. "Of course I can."

"Thank God for that. I was beginning to fear I might be in for a rather grim half hour..."

The barman poured the champagne. He raised his glass "The art of conversation?"

His name was Lal and he had a terrific nerve, but he seemed so friendly it was impossible to take offence. We talked haltingly at first. There was no automatic ease as there had been with Rikh because I soon learned that we shared no great ideals and certainly no worthy intellectual pursuits. He thought that the India League was an abomination and an independent India would be the "triumph of the little man, a victory for the mediocre." I couldn't have disagreed more and I told him so. He might have been the most gorgeous thing on two legs, but I wasn't going to jettison all my principles for a glass of champagne. Not even with him. He listened politely for a while to my Krishna derived arguments—then interrupted me.

"You sound like a barrister." He made it sound like an insult.

"Is that a bad thing?" Frankly, I was flattered.

"Appalling. Dreadful bunch. Barely human."

I must have looked aghast. Nearly all the people I most respected in the world were barristers. Then he mellowed and said, "Take no notice. Sour grapes. Failed the Bar exam, you see."

He grinned as if it were a naughty prank. "Have you ever been to India?"

I shook my head. He looked at me gravely. For the first time it did seem a colossal cheek to be pronouncing on the future of a place I had never even seen.

"Well, I think that when you do and I hope you will, you'll find the reality a lot more complex than you imagine."

I felt put down, but he didn't let me feel uncomfortable. He talked easily and with humour about his family who were many and quarrelsome, going to public school and university so far from home, how he would in the end have to go back "to rule the roost, that is until your chums do away with it." Then he told me he had volunteered for the RAF because he already had a private plane at home in India and, therefore, a pilot's license, and he wanted to make sure that he "did his bit and was in the thick of it" when war came, which we both felt was likely to be very soon.

We drank the champagne and then walked down the Strand. He offered to take me dancing at the Embassy, but I refused because I had no appropriate dress. I was still wearing my business suit and people wore evening dress in those days. He didn't seem to think it mattered. "We could pick up a dress for you. Somewhere on the way?" I refused. After all, I hardly knew him.

So he took me to dinner at the Savoy Grill, which thrilled me because Vivian Leigh was sitting two tables away. I couldn't take my eyes off her, but luckily he could. They were firmly fixed on me.

Afterwards we walked along the Embankment watching the lights reflected in the dark water. He loved London, he said. "So do I," I ventured. "Ah, but yours is the love of a native, isn't it? Whereas mine is that of a stranger passing through. Intense but fleeting." He looked a bit sad at that. We talked for a bit longer and then I went home.

He came to find me the next day. "Ferreting" me out of my office, announcing we would spend the day together. I protested. I told him he'd get me the sack. He shook his head. He had "sorted it all out" with the General Manager, he said. He had asked if the Special Assistant could assist him for a few days with all his business matters, equipping himself for the Air Force, arranging funds to be sent from India and so forth—all with a lordly charm that didn't brook rebuttal and the GM had agreed with a bow and an obsequious smile. Yes, Sir, of course Sir, three bags full, Sir. And the three bags full was me. I told him, he had a hell of a nerve. Prince or not. And had he ever thought to ask me before he arranged for the GM to pimp me in such a manner?

His smile died away. "Do you mind?"

"Not the point," I replied.

"Very much the point I'd have thought." And I was scuppered there because I didn't actually mind at all. In fact I was thrilled, but I wasn't going to let him see that. I didn't want to become another notch on his belt, of which I was sure there were many.

"Look, if you hate the idea, all you have to say is no." There was a silence while I tried to think of a way out of the hole I had dug myself into.

"You look lovely when you frown. I had a governess who frowned like that. Miss Batt she was called. Made me cauliflower cheese and tapioca pudding when I was ill, in the height of an Indian summer. I adored her."

Trouble was, I was beginning to adore him. I put my jacket on.

"Oh, you will come!" He looked radiant at the thought, like a delighted child. I didn't stand a chance.

We spent the day walking round London and talking. In Bond Street he took me to a very exclusive dress shop and bought me a dress to dance in. White chiffon, just like Greta Garbo's. It was exquisite and it cost the earth. He was terribly thoughtful like that. His gifts and treats were never just thoughtless extravagance, but always tailored to the dreams of the recipient. He got my number all right.

He took me dancing at the Embassy Club that night. I was in awe of the place because the Prince of Wales had taken Mrs Simpson there. I would never have dreamed of setting foot in there, but he was a regular. We danced and then he took me to supper at Ciro's where we had oysters and champagne.

He was such fun. Full of energy and life. We had so little in common, nothing really but our youth and laughter. We packed so much into those few days. He had a car—a low sports model, a Bentley, I think. He said it was a mechanical racehorse. He knew a lot about race horses. He had a stud farm in Montgomery and he told me all about it. Which horses ran best on what ground and why. Blood lines. That sort of stuff. A bit lost on me, but fascinating. Another world.

The next day, we drove around London, he ordered his uniform at Gieves and Hawkes, his shoes at Lobbs and we spent hours arranging his funds in the Standard Chartered Bank in Lower Regent Street. Then he took me to tea at Gunters, as a reward he said. Later we dined and danced again, and on that third magical night together we watched the dawn come up. Standing on a deserted Waterloo Bridge.

I shivered in the cold air but would not get back into the car.

"You love it, don't you?"

"Earth hath nothing to show more fair."

He looked puzzled, then twigged.

"Wrong bridge, right sentiment. Wordsworth. He can't have seen you then." He leaned across and kissed me.

On the following night I dressed for dancing, but he took me to the opera instead. I'd told him that I loved it, but never went because it was so expensive. We sat in a box at the Royal Opera House and saw 'Tosca' which I adored. He slept through most of it, uncomfortably perched on his little gilt chair. When it was over and the deafening applause woke him, he joined in. "Marvellous, wasn't it?"

"You were fast asleep!"

"No. Just concentrating." And he clapped extra hard, yelling "Bravo!" at the top of his voice, then he whispered in my ear

"We do get dinner now, don't we?"

"Oh I don't know. It's very late."

"Angel, have a heart. You can't subject a chap to four years of Tosca, sitting on a shooting stick and then deny him dinner. Your human rights friends would have something to say about that."

"Persecution of the princes?"

"Yup. We're a dying breed. Like tigers only less smelly."

He took me to dinner and I was in heaven. We went to a restaurant in Knightsbridge, all red plush, soft lights and gilt mirrors, where we had pheasant and game chips and then glorious Crepes Suzette flambéed at our table in a little copper pan. It was the best evening of my life. He was superb. Mischievous and funny, gentle and attentive. It was bliss.

I stayed with him that night, tip-toeing along the hotel corridor in the early hours, shoes in hand, terrified that someone I knew would spot us. We made love and it was astonishing. A revelation, raw and immediate, yet tender. He was a wonderful lover. He made love as he lead his life—engaged and passionate, intent on his own pleasure yet mindful of mine. He knew that to enhance his own delight he had to share it and he did. In every way, not just in bed. We had such a short time together then, but it was so vivid and intense, the memory of those few days has never faded.

I stayed with him until he left. Trying not to get caught entering or leaving the suite at some ungodly hour, ducking in to doorways to avoid being seen by George and his bellhops delivering the papers and the polished shoes. Mostly I succeeded, but one morning I was caught trying to close the door quietly so as not to wake him, by Veronica, of all people, who saw me and went scarlet. She never acknowledged me again. The irony of that was not lost on me. I had tried to help her.

After four days he left to join his squadron, which was based somewhere in Scotland. He kissed me goodbye. We tried to put a brave face on it, almost succeeded, then hugged each other long and close.

I said I had only one thing to say to him.

"What's that?"

"Come back."

He grinned. "I'll try."

He kissed me again and then he was gone.

Rikh returned two days later. With a rucksack full of dirty washing and the offer of a job. He had done well. Certainly he seemed very pleased with himself. I was less so. Selfishly. The job was a good one and a house came with it, but the job was in Hatfield and the house in Welwyn Garden City. Rikh was over the moon and wanted to move out of London "within the month." The only snag was me. I was the fly in the ointment. I didn't want to live in Welwyn Garden City. My work and my life were in London. He pointed out that a clerical position in a London hotel was a job, not a career. He felt (with some justification) that a position at De Havilland's in Aeronautic Design, affiliated to the Royal Indian Air Force with a starting rank of Flying Officer and commensurate salary, was. You couldn't really argue with that. But I loved my job and my friends and the League and I didn't want to live in complete isolation, cut off from everyone I knew and cared about in some dreary old dormitory town, miles away from everything. Besides, how would Lal ever find me again if I was buried in the country? I had always lived in London, in the centre of things, I said rather pompously.

Predictably he lost his temper.

"This is not a topic for discussion." I wondered if he'd been taking lessons from Krishna. His voice was clipped, its tone final. I tried again. Setting out my arguments and the feelings they contained, only to have them all swept away, dismissed without consideration as "silly and immature." After what felt like hours of circulatory wrangling he pronounced,

"We will be moving to Welwyn."

That did it. Who was this royal "we"? I think I may have asked.

Then he told me that he had already accepted both the job and the house. That we would be living in it "within the month."

"Over my dead body." I replied. I was furious that he had decided my fate without even going through the motions of consulting me. I asked him what made him think he could just make these decisions for me.

"My superior years and intelligence," he replied.

I told him this didn't feel like the exercising of a superior mind. It felt more like a caveman wielding a club. We were supposed to be a modern couple, enlightened, free, the face of tomorrow. An equal partnership, I said. What had become of all that?

Then he really lost his temper.

"What more do you want of me, Nita? I do everything I can for you. What more do you want?" I wished I knew. His voice cracked as he went on.

"I look after you. I pay for you. I encourage you to

expand your mind. I take you out all the bloody time because you can't or won't cook. I put up with the opprobrium of your mother and your friends. (That was too much.He was over-egging it a bit there. Mother wouldn't have dared express opprobrium, even if she'd felt it.) What more do you bloody want?"

How could I possibly tell him?

"The moon and stars?"

Alas, yes. And what's more in the last week I'd had them. But by now Rikh had had enough. Muttering about "not being dependent on moods and megrims of a stupid little girl," he flounced out, slamming the door behind him. Unfortunately, he slammed it so hard that Mrs Lomasney's painted china vase fell off the shelf and shattered on the floor.

I swept it up, feeling completely numb. It seemed symptomatic of our life together somehow. Begun in such bright hope and now in pieces.

He returned some hours later. Calm, rational and cold. I still just felt numb. Not quite ready to move on, but somewhere deep inside not caring.

We patched it up. Neither of us wanted to say goodbye at that point, so we hung on, clinging to the wreckage, as it were. And that spring and summer, with Europe on the brink of war, we hid our heads in the sand and pretended we couldn't see what was coming; at home or abroad. In April conscription was introduced. By August the Germans had signed the Pact of Steel with Italy and a non-aggression Pact with Russia. We and the French guaranteed Poland's sovereignty. It was only a matter of time. We all knew it.

I stuck to my guns. I refused to give up my job. Rikh tore into me with scorn, arguing that I was a pathetic child, hiding behind my friends' skirts, too "scaredy cat" to get a job on my own. He may have had a point. But there was so much I loved about the Waldorf especially that summer—its froth and glamour, the ever changing kaleidoscope of guests. It was perhaps a "la-la land of the simple minded," as Rikh called it, but it was a very seductive one. And besides, it was the place where I had met and loved Lal. And that I was not willing to part with.

I ached with longing for him. I hoped with all my heart that one day he would come back. I would wake up in the endless night beside Rikh and go to the loo on the landing and cry. I longed to have his warm, strong arms around me again, for the sharp masculine smell of his sweat, and the feel of his hair which was long and had never been cut. It reached halfway down his back and was as soft and silky as a child's.

He had been self-conscious about taking his turban off at first. He was worried it would faze me, it had others apparently. Not me. Not for a second. There was no mistaking his sex. I cherished the memory of his smile, the sound of his voice, recalling our conversations over and over, wishing that he would write to me. But he did not.

And life with Rikh now seemed so dreary, so second-rate. Lal wore his youth and rank lightly. He viewed life with a kind of fond amusement, he had fun and while I was with him, so did I; I laughed more in those few days with him than I ever had before. Poor old Rikh, who was permanently losing both his hair and his temper, how could he compete with this dazzling peacock of a man?

I had thought I would not tell anyone about Lal. I wanted to keep it to myself. Our brief magical time seemed so infinitely precious, I didn't want to share it. I wondered if my mother's time with my father had been like this. For her sake, I hoped so.

But over coffee with Yolanda, as usual, I cracked and told her everything. She listened sympathetically, then leaning over to pour us some more coffee, said, "Yeah. I know. The Prince."

I think my jaw actually fell open. I thought we had been so discreet. She laughed.

"Don't look so dismayed. You spent the night with him here, stupida. I don't think there's anyone in the Waldorf who doesn't know."

"Oh." I was not far off tears. She softened her stance.

"He did look rather wonderful." Was she envious?

"He is."

"Then don't you think you should leave Rikh?"

I said nothing, wondering how I could ever explain the mess I was in, even to her.

"You are, after all, madly in love with another man."

Again silence. I couldn't find the words. I didn't have to flounder long, she got swiftly back to business.

"He is all wrong for you, cara mia, you need someone like Lal, not this oriental Polonius. A lover, J, not a father."

Cruel but true. She had started calling people by their initials now.

"Coraggio! Strike out on your own. You don't need old Gruff and Grim."

With that she got up and went back to her office, leaving me with a rapidly cooling coffee and the even chillier knowledge that she was probably right.

Mother, who did not know about Lal, listened in silence when I told her about the Welwyn job and my refusal to give up the Waldorf. She sipped her sherry and her only comment was that it didn't bode too well for the future if we didn't even want to live in the same place. She had never liked him either.

In the end Rikh and I muddled on, papering over the widening cracks in our relationship and at last we hit on a compromise that pleased neither of us very much.

Rikh would accept the job but not the house ("At first," he said rather ominously). We would keep the flat and he would commute part of the week and stay in a B&B recommended by the plant for three nights a week. He would return to me in London for the weekend and for all meetings of the League. I wondered which mattered to him more. It was an uneasy compromise, but for a while it worked.

Chapter Eleven

In the meantime, Mother was moving on, even if I was not. The prospect of another war seemed to have galvanised her somehow, and as ever, decisive and incisive, when she made her moves they were radical.

She started by telling me that she thought it wrong to continue taking money from me when we had not lived together for "some little time" and I "had my own life to lead." I gathered from this that when I first started living with Rikh she had hoped it would not last and I would come back. But now she had given up all hope of that, so she had sold the house on Peel Street and bought herself a new purpose-built flat in Bayswater. She only told me after the deed was done, over our usual sherry at the Cumberland.

I went quiet at that. In truth, I felt a little sad at the passing of my old home. But not very. For me it had never fully moved out of the shadow Cornelius had cast over it—the misery he had sowed there seemed to have penetrated even the bricks and mortar. Long after his death, when Mother had done so much to stamp out the memory of all the unhappy years and fill it with a cheerfulness all her own, I still would sometimes shudder as I put my key into the lock. It was an ingrained reaction. I couldn't help it. But I was sorry that she had not told me of her plans and I said so.

"Oh, I didn't want to churn all that up again. For you or me. A clean break. Always the best way. Never look back, Jeannie, never complain, never explain."

She had moved on all right. She collected up our glasses and took them to the bar. Then she started talking about her flat. Raving about how "convenient" it was, how easy to keep clean, with "everything to hand." And it occurred to me, as always far too late, how lonely she must have been, rattling round in that big old house, full of nothing but memories and pain.

When I did see the flat I loathed it. I went to tea one Saturday straight from the League and work, and after the palatial size of the Waldorf and the large nineteenth-century windows of the League office, with their views of the broad, flowing sweep of the Thames, it seemed cramped and, well, poky. Everything was not so much to hand as within arms' reach. Even the walls. Its two freshly painted rooms and tiny tiled bathroom and kitchen depressed me; it was modern and convenient, no "nooks and crannies to collect the dust" as she put it, but it was also utterly devoid of character. It was far smaller than Rikh's and my flat. But Mother loved it and for that I was pleased.

She didn't stop there either. One Thursday a few weeks later she arrived after me, which had never happened before. She smiled determinedly at me, sat down and then slowly took off her hat, laying it carefully down on the seat between us. I gasped.

Her long thick, wavy hair, always plaited and wound round her head had been pitilessly shorn and soft brown curls now barely covered her ears. Suddenly, she looked terribly young. Her neck long and slender as a girl's. I remembered with a jolt that she was only eighteen years older than me.

"Mama..." Shock made me revert to childhood. She looked at me as if daring me to disapprove.

She smiled broadly. "Well, I thought..." She took a swig of sherry, aghast at her own boldness, "if you can't beat 'em, join 'em!"

"You look so young."

She put the glass down and went on. "I always had to look older, Jeannie, when you were a bairn. There had to be one adult in your life and it was only ever going to be me. So I did everything I could to look, well... certainly more grown up than I felt."

That was the closest she ever came to admitting that bearing the full weight of responsibility for a child, when she herself was still one, had sometimes overwhelmed her.

"You look beautiful, Mama." She did too. I hugged her. Or tried to. She pushed me away.

"Och, don't be so silly," but I knew she was pleased because she had gone all Scots on me, which she only did in times of high emotion.

After that I knew what I had to do. That week I spent all of my week's wages on her. On a pair of pearl earrings not quite as good as mine, but still lovely. I had to get her something of no practical use whatsoever; something she would never buy for herself.

I presented them to her the following Thursday. When she returned from the bar with our Sherries and sat down, I dropped the small packet in her lap.

"What's that for?" She said suspiciously.

"You. Go on. Open it." She did and went scarlet.

"Oh no, Jeannie, they must have cost the earth."

They had. Almost. I nodded.

She dropped the box on the table as if it was red-hot. "You take them back to the shop, my girl, right away."

"I'll do no such thing." I could do Scots too if I was pushed. I had been taught by a master. She shook her head. "I won't accept it. You save your money."

I was a bit hurt, but not surprised. I knew how thrifty and independent she was and I respected that, but she could also be an awful killjoy. This time I wasn't having it. I left the package untouched. She made no move to retrieve it, leaving it on the table where she had dropped it. But when she went to "powder her nose" before the bus ride home, I slipped it into her shopping bag and hid it carefully among the packets of tea and sugar and soap.

We didn't mention it again, but parted as usual.

The next time I saw her she was wearing them. At first we said nothing, then I ventured casually, "You look very smart."

She did too. She looked lovely with her soft curls and new earrings.

"Oh. You mean my earrings?" I nodded, wondering what was coming next.

"Well," she paused, as if taking stock, "They were a gift." Another pause.

"From a very naughty girl." I remembered Lal then and thought, Mama if only you knew. And, thank God, you don't.

Yolanda too was moving on it seemed. Alternating her refugees and causes for the arms of a young man. A doctor called Derek Bentley. She had met him at the London Hospital in Whitechapel when accompanying one of her non-English speaking waifs. I noticed an indefinable change in her. She was always elegantly dressed, style was in her blood, but now there was a subtle glow about her, like the bloom on a flower. A spring in her step, a secret smile on her lips. New habits. The Senior Service cigarettes and calling everyone by their initials. They came from him.

I met him for the first time one evening at Bertorelli's. Rikh and I arrived late from some meeting at the League, the others had nearly finished eating, so there was a bit of a rush and bustle to order our food and get us some wine. Then, as we settled, I noticed a new face. A fairly handsome face. Seated beside Yolanda. He could not have been more different to her if he had come from Mars. He was tall and thin, with sandy coloured hair, bony wrists and hands that were red and roughened from repeated washing. He wore a worn tweed jacket with leather patches on the elbows. He sat, smoking his Senior Service, hardly speaking at all. Well, he would have been hard pushed to get a word in edgewise with that lot. We were as usual all talking, laughing, shouting; waxing lyrical about some undiscovered writer or artist or fulminating angrily about the latest outrage of the Raj. At one point everyone at the table was talking loudly, except him and me. He was absorbed in listening and I was in trouble with my spaghetti. I never could quite get the knack of that. We caught each others' eye and smiled, quiet conspirators in a sea of sound.

That evening he spoke mostly to Rikh. They got on very well right from the start. I think Derek appreciated Rikh's rational intelligence, after the operatic fervour of Yolanda and her friends. Certainly Rikh was a lot quieter, which may have been a bit of a relief to Derek. Then a friend of Yolanda, a somewhat neurotic young man, with long Brylcreemed hair and a checked shirt, was holding forth about the oncoming conflict, censorship and the plans that he claimed had already been secretly put in place.

A government conspiracy to gull the people into acquiescence, he said—lambs to the slaughter, he claimed, just like the Great War. He was a bit drunk; I think he thought he was Wilfrid Owen. Whoever he was, his argument meandered around. Derek listened politely and then chipped in. He spoke quietly, but with authority. He said that was absolute nonsense, that there was very little that was secret about it; plans, for example, were already in place to evacuate the greater parts of all major London hospitals. Only the too sick to move would remain in London, the "mildly sick" had already being sent home and the chronically ill moved to hospitals in the Home Counties. But this was far from being a secret conspiracy, it was common knowledge, he said.

"They have been removed so they cannot protest," ventured the young man, waving his wineglass wildly.

Derek gave a wry smile that died before it reached the edges of his mouth.

"You've a very odd idea about what goes on in a hospital ward. Patients have been moved to make room for air raid casualties. In frighteningly large numbers."

He went on to cite the numbers of extra beds that were being created in London alone, and he described how the previous night he had walked through, the now deserted, wards of his own hospital, past rows of empty beds; his footsteps loud in the echoing corridors, once so full of sound and motion, now silent and still, waiting for the horror to come.

We all fell silent at that. What had been a theoretical argument, an amorphous nightmare, was taking shape around us. War was coming soon. A war that would be played out not just with armies and acts of daring do, but with bombs and ruined cities. I wondered how many of us would be alive by the end of it.

At the end of the evening, we parted in sombre mood. But not before Rikh and Derek had formed a certain bond. As the only two present who already had an active role to play in the forthcoming hostilities, they had a silent understanding, a tacit sympathy. Yolanda seemed very pleased by it. We arranged to meet again soon as a foursome.

The next morning at coffee break I told her how impressed I had been by Derek. His quiet, incisive intelligence, the fact he clearly possessed the sharp compassion of the healers' art. I thought he was admirable and I told her so. She beamed at me, blushing, delighted that I had seen how wonderful he was.

We went out together often after that, and I saw how completely Derek had seen past her fragile bravado and sometimes curt pronouncements. He saw a brave young woman, struggling to break with her tradition while trying to find her way in a world that was fast losing its bearings. He saw her great generous heart and he loved her for it.

A few weeks later Yolanda announced her intention of attending Oswald Mosley's Rally at Olympia. We all begged her not to. We knew there would be a vast crowd, attracted more probably by the doomed desire for peace than devotion to the Fascist cause, but the Blackshirts were thugs and had a history of violence.

Rikh was horrified by the whole idea. He pronounced Yolanda insane or suicidal and refused to have anything to do with it. He would not even discuss it. My heart sank to my boots because I realised that whatever my head and reason dictated, my heart would over-rule them both in a second. I could not let her go alone.

As I left, Rikh's parting shot was, "she's insane and you must have a death wish. These people are not playing at this, Nita, they are really dangerous."

I knew he was absolutely right. I was terrified, but I went anyway. When I met Yolanda at the tube station, I saw that she was not alone. Derek was with her. I must have looked surprised because his greeting was accompanied with an ironic grin and a shrug of his tweed-clad shoulders.

We had arrived at Olympia late and even so, the crowd was was already so immense that it took us an hour to get in, even with tickets. It was the first and only time in my life I had ever been in such a huge gathering. The Fascists proudly boasted afterwards that 30,000 people had attended and it had been touted as the 'world's' largest indoor political meeting." Whether it was that or not, I couldn't say, what I can say is that it made my blood run cold. We watched in silence as ranks of banner waving, drum rolling fanatics in uniform marched in an endless procession into the hall and a substantial number of those present rose to their feet, roaring their approval and raising their arms in the Fascist salute.

Derek, not wishing to "swell Mosley's coffers" had bought the shilling tickets, so we were right at the back and practically in the ceiling. Stunned and appalled, we listened to the tiny, ranting figure far beneath us on the podium, surrounded by his ersatz army. He spoke for about an hour without notes or seemingly a pause for breath. He was listened to in complete silence.

Then a voice piped up beside me. Yolanda, swimming against the tide, shouting her defiance in a wilderness of hate. But not for long.

Two Blackshirts standing in the central aisle grabbed her and dragged her to the back of the hall. I screamed and tried to move towards her, but I was pushed aside. As one of the thugs raised his arm to hit her, it was seized from behind and twisted with surgical precision. He fell to the floor, howling with pain. The other stared in horror.

Derek took Yolanda and me by the arm and marched us smartly towards the exit as if he were steering a couple of dowagers across a dance floor. He barely broke a sweat. At the door he turned and said to the recumbent thug, "That arm's dislocated. You'd better get someone to take a look at it."

The Fascists looked at him in shock and what may have been awe. Then the door banged behind us.

"Run," Derek commanded. We did. We almost fell down the flights of stairs, out onto the street and sprinted down the road and around a corner. Then, breathless and leaning against a wall, holding her side with stitch, Yolanda looked at him and began to laugh.

"You..." she was too breathless to get the words out. Then she began to laugh, but her laughter soon turned to tears and he took her in his arms.

"Are you all right, darling?" I laughed at that. I think we were hysterical... with fear, relief, and astonishment at the cool heroism of this extraordinary man. Then, more firmly, "Y, are you okay?"

She laughed through her tears and clung to him as if drowning. I looked away as they embraced. I don't think anyone had ever defended Yolanda before. I don't think she would have let them. Partly because I don't think she ever acknowledged the real danger her political activities put her in. But Derek was different. His feet were firmly on the ground.

After that, she adored him. She also listened to him, which was rare. As their love grew, I saw how dependent she'd become on him and that level of trust for her was very rare. I had never seen it before. Not with me or her family. Yolanda had always been a curiously solitary figure, even at school or among the crowd of her adult friends, of whom there were many, she existed on her own lonely height. Until now. The goddess was climbing down from her pedestal, and although fearful and tentative, she was glad to be doing so. I rejoiced for her. Delighted that she had found someone worthy of her love who could return it. She was happy. Of that there was no doubt. Their love seemed a bitter contrast to my own increasingly chilly union.

All summer long, London was a buzzing hive of activity. People rushed hither and thither—plans were made for the large scale evacuation of children and the elderly; huge trenches scarred the London parks, sandbags were filled to the delight of the kids, who built elaborate castles in the, as yet, unbagged sand; blackout curtains were put up and gas masks distributed. And still, it all had an air of unreality. A giant masquerade with a cast of millions. All pulling together in a ghastly parody of the Lambeth Walk: all of us Pearly Kings and Queens, cheeky chappies coping, waiting for a war of annihilation.

Until a bright sunny morning in September when the lugubrious tones of Neville Chamberlain, a man we had come to despise in a way that seems horribly unjust now, informed us that we were at war with Germany.

Warsaw was already being bombed. In the next few weeks we watched aghast as the Nazis overran Poland, re-drafting the rules of war. Blitzkrieg: war in which nothing and no-one was spared. No prior rules of conduct were observed. This was a modern war fought with a cruelty that no-one but H G Wells had ever envisaged. The Nazis were teaching us exactly what we could expect.

Winston Churchill, a man I had always loathed because of his total opposition to any form of self-rule for India, became the man of the hour. In purple yet strangely succinct prose, he grasped our situation and put it into words. Words that themselves became history. He knew exactly what we were up against and he knew that whatever the cost we could not lose. It was an odd relief to have it said out loud. Single-handed, he dragged the monster in the corner out of the shadows and forced us to look at it. It was almost too late.

Chapter Twelve

The day war was declared was a Sunday. Rikh and I listened to the broadcast in silence. Then as always, when my world was shaken to its core, I went to see Mother. More unusually, on this occasion Rikh came with me. On the way to the bus stop he bought a handful of newspapers and spent most of the day hidden behind them, but he was there with us. And that was a comfort. I remember that the streets were strangely deserted, eerily quiet, but it was a lovely day, sunny and warm.

We were all overwrought, but pretending to be normal. Mother seemed composed and unflappable, but her hands shook as she beat the eggs into the cake mix and she burned her arm on the oven door. I wondered how she had felt and where she had been when the last war was declared. I didn't dare ask. I excused myself by thinking that I couldn't really ask her something like that with Rikh present, but the truth was that it was unlikely I would have anyway. So I slipped right back into my old role of Number One Helper, no questions asked, and clattered about, dropping the knives and forks as I laid the table.

It was a strange day. Punctuated by brief announcements on the wireless and long, uneasy silences. Not one of us dared say what we felt. I felt strangely detached. I looked across the box-like confines of Mother's sitting room, and saw Rikh avidly reading the papers, trying to make sense of the tidal wave that would surely carry him so far from everything he had hoped for. It was inconceivable that India would be granted independence or any degree of autonomy while we were at war. Then I remembered that Rikh was a serving officer in a colonial air force and his life was at much at risk as any British born airman. He was trapped now, with no way home. The bitter truth was that he could die defending that which he most hated. The irony of this was not lost on me, and I felt a huge wave of tenderness for him, especially when I noticed that despite his calm, almost severe exterior, the usually dapper Rikh had forgotten to brush his hair over his bald spot and was wearing odd socks. I felt a pang of remorse that I had not looked after him better. For all our troubles, he was, at that moment, infinitely dear to me.

And Mother? As I watched her bustle about, cooking, preparing, looking after us, if not calm then always capable, she meant so much to me that even the thought she might come to harm made my heart race. I felt I couldn't breathe. So I did what she did. Banished the thought that disturbed me and got on with it. Her everyday courage had always moved me, but you could also call it sweeping it all under the carpet. Both were true.

We ate the lunch she made for us. And after she and I had cleared the table, she suggested we play cards. And so we did. An unlikely trio. Even Rikh joined in to my astonishment. We played cribbage, I seem to recall, and Rikh won which surprised no-one.

Mother laughed when he won for the fifth time and said she would play no more.

"I know when I'm beaten," she said, but she was smiling and even managed to evoke a rare smile in return from Rikh.

"I'll put the kettle on." She was getting up but Rikh stopped her.

"No, Elizabeth, I'll make the tea," he announced with the air of a Rockefeller distributing millions. And he did. Rikh's tea was what I had come to call Krishna's tea. Scalding hot (he boiled it all up in a pan, including the milk), very sweet and so strong you could stand the spoon up in it. Mother sipped, winced but said, "Well! A good strong cup of tea. Just what the doctor ordered. Now who's for cake?"

She kept running her tongue across her teeth, trying to get rid of the tannin coating.

"In for a penny..." Rikh was really trying. When she

went out to get the cake I gave him a quick kiss on the forehead.

"Thanks," I whispered. And he just smiled and for a second I thought I had the old Rikh back.

Mother came bustling in with the cake on a tray and her best china.

"Last time we all thought it would be over by Christmas. Let's hope this one will be."

With that she opened Mrs Lomasney's carved oak sideboard and took out her Christmas bottle of sweet sherry. I saw Rikh's eyes open wide and hoped this would not be a step too far.

"We'll drink a toast." She poured the sweet syrupy liquid into Mrs Lomasney's beautiful tulip shaped glasses.

"Here's tae us—wha's like us? Damn few!" The old Scots toast. I had known it all my life, but it was new to Rikh and he warmed to it, standing and raising his glass to Mother. I didn't tell him the last line "And they're aw died," I thought it might mar the moment.

I was just happy they were getting on, but on the way home the barrage balloons—thirty or forty of them—were rising slowly into the darkening sky, like great silver clouds. An air raid siren sounded and the bus stopped. A policeman rode by on a bicycle, shouting "Take cover!" but nobody knew where. The streets were full of people, standing in their doorways, staring up at the sky, wondering what would happen next. After a little while the bus took off with a jolt and we arrived home safely.

Nothing happened, but London was changing. The bulky balloons crowded the graceful spires and roof tops and the dense darkness of the first blackout took us by surprise. London was wearing a completely different face. She was arming herself for war. I felt the first cold shiver of fear. This was just the beginning—what would be left of the city I knew and loved by the end? We spent the rest of the evening in silence.

Things were even changing at the Waldorf. A few weeks after the declaration of war, Freddy came into my office at about eleven. I thought he had come for coffee and a chat as usual, so I didn't even look up but carried on carefully inking in the pencilled figures in the ledger book. You had to be awfully careful of nib pens or the ink smudged.

He said nothing at first, which was odd. Freddy liked to chat. He could always be relied upon to be up to date with the latest gossip. Betty at reception used to laugh at him and say that he would get wind of any whiff of scandal before it had even happened. She used to call him the "blood-hound". And he was always bursting to spread the news. So, as the silence remained unbroken, I looked up. Freddy was red-faced and sweating. It seemed to me he was swaying. I looked more carefully: Freddy was drunk.

"'S'war," he announced dramatically, slurring his words. Now Freddy was always very careful with his diction. He didn't want his origins betrayed. There were many people like that then, desperate not to be found out. It made me smile. I, who had so much to hide, could always spot them because their deliberate over-enunciation, particularly of vowels, gave their speech a contrived, genteel quality that was unmistakeable.

"Yes," I said. What else could I say? I was trying to help him out, but I hadn't a clue what he was driving at.

"S'the finish of everything," and with that he fell into the chair, his head lolling like a broken doll.

"Freddy, are you drunk?"

"No." He shook his head emphatically. "Maybe li'l bit."

I sighed. "For God's sake, Freddy! The GM will kill you if he finds you like this. Go to the gents and freshen up. I'll get you some coffee." I stood up.

"S'no good, s'too late," he wailed. He tried to stand.

"What are you on about?" Half-standing and swaying alarmingly, he pulled a crumpled letter out of his pocket and brandished it in front of my face.

"S'all over. Waldorf, new job, Ruislip, everything." Falling back into the chair with a thud. I snatched the letter from him. I wondered for a moment if Veronica had given him the push.

She hadn't. It was his call-up papers—telling him that in accordance with the Armed Forces Act (1939) he was called upon for service and should present himself at the Albany Street Barracks in two days' time. Poor old Freddy, he had hung on with us an extra month to enable the GM to train his successor and now he would never have the chance to follow his dream.

"Y'see," he wailed. I did.

"King and Country. Gotta go, gonna die in a ditch like those poor sods on the Somme." He was howling at full throttle now.

"Not if the GM gets you first. For God's sake, Freddy, shut up!" He was making such a racket, Yolanda came out of her office to see what was going on.

Together we poured pints of strong, black coffee into him until he had recovered enough to stand up. Apparently, George had had a bottle of whisky hidden away and had decided to drown Freddy's sorrows as well as his own. It was all very well for George, he hardly ever stood up anyway.

As soon as Freddy could stand, we frogmarched him out of the building and propped him up at his bus stop. God knows how he got home. We told the GM he had been "taken ill, suddenly, you know, gyppy tummy," we explained, praying he was on that bus and not wandering back.

The GM looked mournful. He said we would have to get used to managing without Freddy or his replacement very soon anyway. He said a large number of the male staff of conscription age would be going. Across the board, he said. Waiters, porters, maintenance. He didn't know how we were going to manage, he said miserably. Then he went into his office and shut the door.

"Silly old fool. A world at war and all he's worried about is that some old Doris will have to carry her own case." Yolanda muttered as she marched back to her desk, as if ready to tackle the Wehrmacht single-handed. Darling Y, she was an absolute Valkyrie—only you wouldn't dare tell her, cos she'd have killed you.

Within a few days Freddy was gone. I was surprised how much I missed him. He had befriended me when I first came and punctuated my working day with his chatter, his endless love of gossip, his soppy opinions, gleaned straight from the Daily Mail, and his sudden bursts of boyish laughter. The days seemed dull and suddenly very long without him. I wasn't the only one who missed him. Veronica walked the corridors of the Waldorf with set jaw and red eyes, but still refused to even acknowledge my sympathetic smiles and attempts at conversation. She was a grim old bat, but she loved him and clearly missed him very badly. We all did. The GM especially. Freddy's trained up replacement Sydney Fowle, was useless, but thankfully he was soon gone too.

The Waldorf was gradually becoming denuded of young men. Most of the waiters in the dining room were replaced by "women" to the horror of the maître d'. George even had to face the prospect of female bellhops—whom he regarded with horror. They clustered around him in the lobby, in their swiftly run-up, ill-fitting uniforms, anxious to do well. George wanted nothing to do with them. He either snubbed them completely or was incredibly rude, reducing them to tears with his non-stop rant about the uselessness of "women, everywhere like vermin," then poured scorn on them for weeping. "That's right, pipe your eyes, it's all you're good for." Several times, overhearing this, Yolanda had to be restrained from slapping him. But we all watched aghast when some elderly favourite would arrive, laden with the shipping trunks and heavy studded cases of yesteryear, and George, lumbering, limping George, would leap into life and execute a neat rugby tackle, knocking bell girls out of the way, to haul the bags and keep the princely tip he knew would be his. Otherwise, he didn't bother, he just let them struggle and sniped from the sidelines.

He was drinking all the time now. The bottle clinking in his pocket. "Dutch courage," he would slur if caught tippling. "Want some?" I'm ashamed to say that sometimes we did. "You can look askance, Missy," he growled at Betty when she recoiled in the face of his boozy breath, "you don't know what you're in for. I went through the last one. Got the gammy leg to prove it." And he weaved off across the foyer like an old bear, broken but still snarling.

Despite the disappearance of large numbers of men, the early evacuation of some women and many children, an air of unreality still permeated London. The Phony War. The imminent gas attacks, the mass air raids and casualties had, as yet, failed to materialise. The blackout covered every window, every source of light from the grandest chandelier to the humblest torch was dimmed and at night we stumbled around in the unused to darkness, falling off curbs and losing our way home, while wardens patrolled the sand-bagged streets and the silver barrage balloons bobbed above our heads like grotesque Christmas decorations.

But the all-out war we had been told to expect from day one had not reached us yet. A sense of waiting for the worst to come hung heavily over us all and was then replaced by a kind of blithe acceptance. Theatres and cinemas closed, to my relief. No more trailing across London to sit for hours on a wooden bench. But the pubs were still open and did a roaring trade. George was right after all. Booze oiled the wheels and kept fear at bay, or at least drowned it, in a kind of brittle bravado. It was a cold winter 1939/40 and coal was scarce. So we huddled together in each others' homes; and, as the feared onslaught failed to come, with spring London slowly opened up again.

We went to the cinema often then, even Rikh relenting and accompanying me when he could. I remember 'Ninotchka' was a great favourite of mine. I went with him and then again with Yolanda. From time to time, when home alone, with Rikh away on duty in Hatfield, I would open the drawer and take out the white chiffon dress Lal had given me. I never wore it for anyone else, but I would run its soft, cloudy folds through my fingers—a dreamlike dress for a dreamlike time. Lal seemed hardly real to me now; his face, the loving and laughter, now slipped through my memory, as elusive and ephemeral as the cloth itself. Beautiful but barely there.

Chapter Thirteen

Rikh had graduated to flying ops now. At first, we had both assumed he would be a backroom boffin, solely occupied with aeronautics and new design. Essential war work, but comparatively safe. Then one evening, he came home early. He was waiting for me, sitting at the scarred oak table in the kitchen, a cold cup of tea untouched in front of him. He was staring into the distance, one elbow on the table, resting his face in his hand.

"Penny for them?" I put the shopping down on the draining board. It wasn't a very inspiring clutch, some rather ancient looking potatoes and a hunk of very fatty bacon, and not too much of either. I was preoccupied, wondering how I could turn this unappetising mix into an evening meal. I took my coat off. He still said nothing.

"Rikh, are you okay?" He turned and looked at me. "I've been put on ops. Going to Scotland next week for flight training." I wondered for one panic stricken second if he'd meet Lal. Then it hit me.

"They can't do that. You're a designer, a backroom guy."

"That was the idea. But it's not that kind of war. It's the all hands on deck kind. There are so few pilots, you see. And I did have a few flying lessons back home, years ago."

I sat down before my legs gave out under me. The two men I had ever loved would now be in the air above England, risking their lives, one fighting for an Empire he had come to hate and the other desperate to preserve it.

"Oh Rikh..." I could hardly breathe, let alone speak.

But Rikh had pulled himself together. "So, it has occurred to me that we should marry."

I was shocked, horrified.

"Why?" I said, "I thought we were above all that. A union of choice, not law. Bohemians."

"I know but if anything happens to me... you might be better off."

"Oh Rikh, no!" What was I refusing to countenance, marriage with a man I no longer loved whole-heartedly, or the prospect of his death?

He smiled bleakly. "Too late. I've already bought the license."

As ever I was to have no choice in the matter. What was best had been decided and not by me.

"We'll do the deed on my return from Scotland. Now, what's this?" He peered into the shopping bag and grimaced.

"No. Not tonight. Put your coat on. We'll go out."

I did as I was told. I remember walking out of the house and waiting for the bus. Then the tiny restaurant in Soho with the guttering candle on a chipped saucer; the battery acid wine we drank too much of. Not much else. Except at one point during the meal, he took my hand and smiled tenderly.

"Poor little baby, so inexperienced, so absurdly young." I could feel my cheeks burning. Not half as young and inexperienced as he thought. I felt so sorry that night. Sorry that the War had turned him into a fighter, he who loathed the very idea of war; sorry that all that was left of the great rush of love we had felt at first was a mutual regard and a kind of detached affection. We gazed into each other's eyes, thinking so much and saying so little, pitying each other, mainly for being involved with the other one.

It was a funny thing—the thought of possible demise brought us closer together. At that time what held us together was greater than that which divided us. Or was it just that the prospect of losing what you have, however flawed, makes you value it? At one point, Rikh even said as much:

"There's nothing like the fear of extinction to make you cherish being alive."

It never occurred to me then that he might be frightened. Cool, rational Rikh? Never. It does now.

He became kind and protective, and a lot less angry. Or

perhaps he now had another object for his wrath. And I saw a man who had tried to battle with Titans—defying both sets of conventions, breaking with tradition whilst trying to set a sub-continent free, taking me on. I now think the man should have got the George medal just for that. For Valour. Certainly. He was a brave man. We loved each other dearly, but not enough. It was not his fault he could not win every battle, could not measure up to a man who was in many ways his inferior, a man who lacked his breadth of vision but who had a capacity for love.

Then came Dunkirk and our survival was very much in question. Depicted in the press as a triumph (and it was hard not to thrill with pride as the nation rescued the army. I was not immune to that and I was happy those boys were saved), but the cold, hard truth was very different. It had been a rout: we had been kicked out of Europe by the Germans, who were now invincible and poised to invade.

We were married in the summer of 1940. Just before Rikh departed for ops, while the Battle of Britain raged in the sky above. Our wedding was a quiet, subdued affair. We wanted and could afford no more. Rikh wore a rather splendid dark suit, borrowed from Krishna, which was far too big for him. I wore my, now quite worn, business suit, a severe black, only relieved by the beautiful white silk blouse that was a present from the Barronis. It had an antique lace collar and cuffs and Mama Barroni, with Yolanda's help, had carved up her wedding dress to make it. I wore my pearl earrings and a tiny blue gentian brooch, made of carved wood that Mother had given me. She presented it with tears in her eyes and tight, pursed lips, thrusting it at me as if the touch of it burned her. She said, "something blue. Only thing your father ever gave me. I want you to have it." She turned away, her hurt like a palpable being between us. The least I could do was wear it. For her. Him I cursed roundly. Not for the first time. But I have it still.

We were a motley crew at the reception. Betty and Syd Fowle came from the Waldorf. The GM declined our invitation, but sent me a beautiful orchid corsage which was most unexpected and generous, although I did suspect that Yolanda had a bullying hand in it. Friends from the League came with Krishna who wore his second best suit, Rikh having purloined his best, and an air of benevolent disdain. Freda, Mother's best friend from our Peel Street days. And, of course, my beloved Barronis. They arrived heavily laden with bottles of champagne, delicious food, and the love and laughter that accompanied them everywhere. Papa B sweating a little, tightly buttoned into a heavy three piece suit with spats for the occasion, and Mama B resplendent in her magenta silk and diamonds.

Mother did not come to the registry office. She said she was too busy with the reception which was held in her tiny flat, despite the Barronis' offer of a restaurant venue. Uncle Vittorio's, I suspect. Mother had refused that point-blank and they backed down gracefully, acknowledging that it was her call. I would have preferred Uncle Vittorio's frankly, but my wishes didn't seem to come into this at all.

So while we "did the deed" as Rikh called it, Mother stayed at home, making the light and airy lemon curd tarts that only she and I knew had always been my childhood favourite. She had bought flowers and sherry and made cakes. When I asked how she ever got hold of the sugar and butter and eggs for such a feast, she smiled and answered "I work in a restaurant, Jeannie. Do you think I have no friends?" She must have had incredible friends to get all of that, and she was already a master at turning a little into a lot. She'd had a lifetime's practice, after all, and she didn't let me down that day.

Yolanda and Derek were our witnesses. Yolanda had spent most of the previous evening trying to persuade me not to go ahead with the wedding. Friends at the League had organised a strange, booze free (or so they said), stag night for Rikh, and Yolanda came to the flat to set my hair for me and help me "pretty up" as she called it. She set my hair with the metal clips we used in those days, pinching my reluctant locks into the waves and curls that were fashionable then and painting my nails for me. All the while, subjecting me to a non-stop barrage along the lines of "don't do it, you know it's not right, he's not right, you'll only live to regret it." It was dreadful. She was worse than any mother could ever be. I told her so, when we were about three-quarters through the very good bottle of Valpolicella she had brought with her.

I told her we couldn't wait to see what the future would bring, that I hadn't wanted to marry, but I had been talked round because we could all be dead tomorrow. "If you go through with this, you'll wish you were," was her response.

"What will you do if Lal comes back?" She was never one to beat around the bush.

"I don't think he will."

"Do you want him to?"

"Yes." A torrent of feeling, ignored for so long, came flooding out in a rush.

"He never wrote. He promised he would, but he never did. I wrote to him... more than once." The hurt and humiliation felt like acid in my throat.

She looked at me in silence for a while. When she did speak, her voice was gentle. "If you feel like that, you can't go through with this marriage. It's a lie."

"Nothing's that simple anymore. I do love Rikh... but..."

She looked down at my scarlet nails and frowned, then wiped off an imaginary smudge.

"It's not enough, cara, and it never will be."

I took her hand. "Stop it. Don't scold anymore. You made my wedding blouse for me. Why did you do that if you hated the whole thing so much?"

I went on. "Just come with me. I know it's a mess, but it's the war. Everything's a mess; nothing's in the right place anymore. I know you don't approve, but I really need you to be there."

She enveloped me in a tight bear hug, grinding the metal clips into my scalp and spilling the varnish on the rug. I never could get the stain out.

When we arrived at the registry office the next morning she was already there, with Derek. She was smiling, laughing in an impossibly chic silk suit, a deep azure blue, the colour of a Mediterranean sky. A corsage of spring flowers on her shoulder. She put the bride to shame and I loved her for it. My beautiful Yolanda.

The ceremony, far too grand a term for the hurried service and mumbled responses, was brief and ungracious. The officiant had too many weddings these days, he grumbled. He clearly disapproved of Rikh's colour, behaving as if he were about to grant us bail rather than marry us. He was late arriving, rushed headlong through the whole thing and left abruptly, as soon as the business was done. He did not wish us well at any point. I could see Yolanda was furious. She was like a seething pot, ready to boil over. Derek, however, shook his head at her, then practically tripped up the escaping clerk, and said in a loud voice, "Thank you. I'm sure you'll want to wish the happy couple well."

It wasn't a question. It was actually more of an order. But, with an easy authority that brooked no dissent, he forced the clerk into a constricted smile and a reluctant expression of good will. Derek was a force to be reckoned with. You could see what he'd be like in his operating theatre. But he made Rikh smile for the first time that day, and I just felt soppy with love for the pair of them. Rather more than for my groom, in fact.

After that Yolanda ran ahead and showered us with rose petals. "I thought you hated all this," I hissed at her. "I do, but I love you so much more than I disapprove of you. In any case, I'm Italian."

She marched off ahead and we got into Derek's car. We drove back to Mother's flat, where the Barronis greeted us like conquering heroes and showered us with confetti and loud operatic singing of 'For they are jolly good fellows'. Descant and base. I didn't know whether to laugh or cry. Mother was in much the same state. It was a funny old day: laughter and tears, the generosity of friends and the hostility of a stranger. I have often wondered what Rikh made of it. He never said.

We mulled around awkwardly in the tiny little flat. There were few guests, but they easily filled the space. We thanked them all for coming. Mother had already made sure they were amply provided with food and Papa Barroni did the honours with champagne. For a while, it all went swimmingly.

Then Rikh rose to his feet. He waved his glass and called for silence. It occurred to me that he was drunk. Rikh was never drunk and I wondered what had prompted such an uncharacteristic loss of control. Was it relief that the deed had been done or horror as he realised what he was in for? I felt very detached by now; oddly uninvolved, as if I were looking at the scene through a stranger's eyes. I remember feeling quite interested as to what this newly unconstrained Rikh would come out with. I didn't have to wait very long.

He began to speak, addressing himself to his chums from the League.

"Today Juanita and I are joined in matrimony." Yolanda and I exchanged glances.

"And I..." here he waved his glass around a bit, "have undertaken the care and nurture of this vulnerable girl so much my junior..." He looked at me then continued, "a fatherless child, all alone in the world."

Oh God. The Leaguers nodded in approval, his florid speech didn't grate on them: they were used to such language. He went on. Mother was watching him with ominously shining eyes and suddenly flushed cheeks. He went on about me. You'd have thought I was Orphan Annie he'd picked up in the gutter. No mention was made of the parent I did have. The one who was standing right next to him.

He looked at me with a sort of boozy tenderness and started up again.

"I have given my word..." here, he paused for breath. Fatally as it turned out.

"Your word? I have given my life..." It was Mother, all guns blazing. She was like Vesuvius. She erupted rarely, but when she did it was lethal. She swallowed, as if she were choking on his words.

"She is not all alone in this world! She never has been!

I have cared for her since the moment she was born. Always putting her well-being before mine. Can you give me your word you will do the same?"

There was a terrible silence. Rikh just looked silly—deflated, aghast, his upraised glass still in his hand. Mother was unrecognisable—savage, wild, a tigress laying claim to her cub. And I—the meat in the middle—was being torn in two.

In the awkward silence that followed, battle lines were being drawn. Yolanda glared at Rikh, as if she longed to murder him. Mama Barroni moved close to Mother, instinctively taking her side. The Leaguers looked bemused, betraying the cultural gulf between us. How could a woman with no husband or family offer protection? Krishna looked down at his nicely buffed nails, even more scornful than ever.

Then Derek stepped into the breach. He raised his glass and spoke firmly,

"I think we are all agreed that with the loving care of her mother and now also her husband, Juanita is indeed blessed. And we, her friends, rejoice in this and wish them every happiness. Nita and Rikh!"

He didn't give anyone time to respond. A ragged chorus of "Nita and Rikh" went up and they drank to us. However, the two protagonists were all at sea. Rikh was humiliated and Mother, appalled by her outburst, fled into the kitchen with Freda at her heels. It wasn't over then. Derek launched into another somewhat tuneless chorus of

"For they're jolly good fellows." The Barroni family choir kicked in and fortunately they sang well enough to make it sound like a tribute. As soon as she finished, Derek put his arm round Rikh's sagging shoulders and led him away, leaving the non-plussed Leaguers staring after them. Not quite slack jawed, but not far from it.

I wanted to laugh. I always did in moments of tension and the worse the moment the stronger the urge. I couldn't believe it: on my wedding day, they were fighting over me like a couple of dogs with a bone.

Derek obviously placated Rikh with talk of "mothers and daughters, you know, old chap" and "emotions run a bit high on these occasions" and other soothing platitudes, but whatever they were it worked because when they reappeared a few minutes later, Rikh's shoulders were back in the right place and he even managed a weak smile in my direction. His friends then gathered round him, anxious to support him in the face of such an incomprehensible onslaught.

So Derek saved the day. For the second time. Yolanda was looking at him with adoration in her eyes as he moved effortlessly between the clusters of guests, exchanging a joke here, a few words there, a smile elsewhere. The man inspired trust. I didn't know whether he deserved it. I hoped so for Yolanda's sake, but he could pull it out of people like a conjuror with a rabbit.

After a while Mother reappeared. For a time we skirted around each other, not speaking, not even meeting the others' eyes, tense and uneasy, like cats on a fence. I was angry. Rikh could be a bully and a fool, we both knew that, but we also knew he meant well. But Mother... I had expected better from her.

The agony went on. Through champagne and the inevitable sherry, through small mountains of sandwiches and cake, to cups of tea, and an emptying room. Rikh came over and mentioned he thought it was time to go. I took my bag into the bedroom. I didn't have a trousseau or even a going-away dress, but we were going to Salisbury for two nights and I wanted at least to powder my nose.

As I was seated at the spartan dressing table, its plywood drawers covered by a ruffled cotton curtain, I saw Mother in the mirror. She stood behind me, eyes still blazing, flushed and unhappy. Then she said softly,

"I'm sorry to have embarrassed you, Jeannie." It was almost a whisper. I dissolved. I was cross, but I didn't care. I just loved her best always and I told her so. I took her firmly in my arms, astonished that anyone so powerful could be so small. She buried her head in my shoulder, shy as an errant child and whispered, "And I you. All the world." We stood like that for a little while. Then we pulled apart, pulled ourselves together, and brushed, powdered and spruce went back into the living room. I to take my leave of the few remaining guests, and she to resume her role as host. We did it rather well, I thought.

Rikh and I had a wonderful time in Salisbury. We were determined to. We only had two days and we were both adamant that we were going to make the best of it. We had chosen Salisbury because of its antiquity and the Magna Carta. Rikh wanted to see that. I would have preferred the sea, but the coast was out because the beaches were mined.

We drove down in our borrowed car (the same one Rikh had moved me out of the old house in Peel Street). It belonged to Dillip Shah, a barrister in the League, and it was showing its age. It chugged and rattled along like an old train and the leather on the seats was worn thin and even torn in one place, but we didn't care. We were thrilled to have it and even more thrilled by the freedom of movement it gave us; used to the ponderous transport of bus and train, the rigmarole of buying tickets, then waiting for the damn thing to arrive, the notion that you could just get in and go seemed wondrous to us both. And it was terribly kind of Dillip to lend us his car with its precious petrol ration.

By the time we arrived in Salisbury, it was dark and, at first, the Rose and Crown, an old coaching inn, full of shadows and oak beams, seemed a bit forbidding. But even though it was a mild summer evening, there was a roaring fire in the bar and the staff made us very welcome. I had worried about how they would take Rikh, but he'd changed out of Krishna's suit before we left, (Krishna's generosity didn't extend to the honeymoon apparently), and was now back in uniform. That swung it. Hearing that it was our honeymoon and we only had two days before Rikh went on ops, the landlord served us huge whiskies (practically a tumbler full, what I would later learn to call a "Patiala peg") and excused himself for a few minutes. He then ushered us up to a lovely room with a four-poster bed and an en-suite bathroom. It was old and quirky with an uneven floor, and steeply sloping ceiling. Bulging plaster and thick dark timbers, we hoped, held the whole thing together. The floorboards creaked, the bath tap spluttered, the pipes banged and knocked, then groaned rudely and emitted a thin trickle of tepid brown water. The soap was Coal Tar. I think it was their best room. We had a fit of the giggles and pronounced it perfect.

The landlord gave us a wonderful dinner—Brown Windsor soup, and roast chicken. There was even junket for pud, which Rikh loathed but ate with good humour.

We were determined that the row at the reception was not going to spoil our fun. On the way down Rikh had lit a cigarette for me and said quietly,

"I didn't mean to offend her."

"I know. It's just..." How could I ever explain?

"I know. You and she had to be everything to each other. I understand that, but it doesn't make it any easier for someone else to come in..." He drew heavily on his own cigarette, "it can feel like a closed circle."

He spoke in a tentative manner that was unusual for him. I could see his point. There was nothing I could or would do about it, but I did begin to see how awkward and excluding it must be for him. I nodded and said nothing, but decided to be very good to Rikh from now on. For a while I was.

It wasn't difficult to be good humoured in that lovely place. We roamed around the cathedral, marvelling at the delicate beauty of its soaring arches. Then climbed the three hundred odd steps to the spire to look out across the water meadows to the country beyond.

Rikh spent ages in the Chapter House with the Magna Carta. "Aha," he said, as he stood in front of it, as if trying to get a bead on his ancient enemy. "The Great Charter of the Liberties of England," he announced, "but not anywhere else," he muttered under his breath while leaning in for a closer look. Despite his misgivings, it clearly meant a lot to him. "It's so old, Nita, but still so relevant." This new reverence for all things ancient was beginning to grate on me. "Oh? I wasn't aware we were ruled by a load of old barons."

"Don't be flippant. What makes it remarkable is that it legislates that rulers are accountable and can be overruled for the common good."

He was a pompous old stick. But right as ever. So I pinched his bum and told him so.

We drove to Stonehenge, where the massive bulk of antiquity dwarfed us as we walked through the ancient towering stones. We felt sheltered there, small and insignificant, and oddly comforted at being so.

We went for long walks through sunshine and warm summer rain, and drank weak tea in teashops (Krishna would never stand for this, was Rikh's only comment) and warm beer in country pubs. We even made love in our four-poster bed piled high with fat downy pillows. I forced Rikh to have a cream tea. It was like taking a stray cat to the vet because he hated scones, but I pointed out that what with sugar and butter now being rationed his chances of this in the future were going to be mighty few and if he was going to pull down an Empire, he ought to take the trouble to explore its traditions. If only for political expediencey. He laughed at that and humoured me, eating all the butter and jam crammed onto tiny bits of scone, leaving the rest of it in heaps of crumbs scattered around his plate to the tutting annoyance of the waitress.

We drove back into London in the early evening, approaching from the west. Ahead of us, to the east, the city was on fire. Anti-aircraft guns blazed and the sky was raked by searchlights. The planes caught in them looked like toys—but nothing seemed to deflect them: we could see the bombs falling on the docks and still they kept on coming, wave after wave, squadron after squadron. The whole horizon was bright with flames. It was a terrifying sight. An inferno. You could not believe anyone within its compass would be left alive. In a few brief hours, London had become "the greatest target in the world." The Blitz had begun.

Chapter Fourteen

With Rikh away so much now flying ops, I was often alone for weeks at a time.

The local air raid warden lived in our block and he organised a rota of residents to perform fire-watching duties. I took my turn, watching for fires on the flat roof of our building, armed only with a tin hat that was far too big, a set of army binoculars and a pair of keen eyes; hardly the cutting edge of the war effort, but it made me feel I was "doing my bit." If we saw anything we had to run down and get him so that he could alert the fire service "quick sharp."

Perched high up on the roof, scanning the surrounding area for any sign of fire, gave me an overview, an odd kind of detachment. We were bombed quite heavily in our district because the main North/South railway line ran through it. Munitions and heavy armaments came down that route from the factories in the North and Gerry tried to take them out. On a nightly basis, it seemed. Huddled up in a hairy old blanket, with a thermos of tea, I spent whole nights watching the sky. I even quite liked it. I hated the shelters. I used them because I had to, but I felt trapped, crammed in there like sardines in a can, waiting for Gerry to come and finish us off.

During one raid, a bomb came down the air shaft of the Underground station in which many people were sheltering. That was horrific. Yolanda, who had taken a short nursing course and now did her bit at the First Aid Post in Mornington Crescent, had witnessed its aftermath. She came in to work the next morning, white lipped and shaking. At first she couldn't talk at all, she just trembled. Then she gradually opened up. She told me the Post had had to be turned into a temporary morgue; they couldn't dig the people out, only bodies or bits of them, and there were quite a few children among them. She was badly shaken and it took a lot to shake Yolanda. In the end, the GM sent her to one of the unoccupied bedrooms to rest, but when I went up to take her a cup of tea, I found her sitting bolt upright, unable to sleep, despite the purple hoops around her eyes, smoking one cigarette after another and still shaking. I asked the GM what I should do. "Carry on, my dear," he replied, "What else can we do?" He, too, was pale with exhaustion and his pin striped trousers and black jacket hung loose on his newly gaunt frame. He never seemed to go home anymore, but slept in a little cubby space behind his office, ready to defend his sanctuary.

Sometimes there was nothing even the fire service could do and we had to watch helplessly as the fires burnt out of control. Then whole areas, especially in the City, had to be abandoned and the fires left to burn themselves out, wreaking a terrible destruction. Fanned by the wind, they grew and spread, devouring everything. From my eyrie high above, I watched as the bright torches of flame lit up the night sky and turned a living city into a wasteland. A city of ashes where the air smelled of burning and the smouldering fires burned for days. I watched and felt a strange compulsion to remain, to bear witness. A fragment of poetry, learned long ago at school, came back to me. "A tyrant spell has bound me and I cannot, cannot go."

In the end, dizzy with hunger and tiredness, I just felt angry. How dare they? The Wren churches, the medieval Guildhall, the house in Silver Street where Shakespeare had lived and written his plays were not just buildings, they were my history. They had been the landscape of our lives for centuries, an enduring part of who we were. All now utterly destroyed. I hated them for it. Someday there would be a reckoning for this, I vowed. Little did I know.

Rikh was very angry with me. He had wanted me to move to Welwyn right away and was furious when I did not.

"Is there any particular reason why you're so keen to become an air raid casualty?"

"Well, yes. Several actually." I was worn out with this argument. The same row repeated endlessly every time we were together. "There's Mother and Yolanda and my job." I think he actually snorted at that.

"And all our friends and the League. I don't want to cut and run."

He looked at me with contempt. "What a child you are!" And I thought how strange, what had begun as a term of endearment was now a term of abuse. He went on.

"Why this pathetic bid to be the boy on the burning deck?"

His scorn forced me to take refuge in silence. It didn't make me change my mind. There was also the faint but still glimmering hope that I might see Lal again. And something else was dawning in me. Something even I dismissed as silly at first, but which became increasingly important. I had always despised patriotism. I still do. But London was my home and as I walked among her ruins I discovered how much I loved her. I tried to explain this to Rikh, but I found it hard to put into words, and he cut my ramblings short, dismissing it all as "sentimental twaddle."

He even appealed to Krishna, wanting him to lend his weight to the argument and bully me into exile. Krishna heard us both out, then gave his verdict with a wintry smile.

"How can we—of all people—whose love of home is so great it drives us to such drastic and sustained action. How can we despise her for feeling something similar? She cannot cut and run anymore than we can, Rikh. You should not expect it of her."

I was so shocked by this, I burst into tears. Then they both looked at me with scorn. They despised tears.

None of this helped us to get on. It seemed our brief period of rapprochement had been all too temporary, despite our best efforts. Rikh, when he did come home, was grey with tiredness and thoroughly dispirited. He hated war and everything about it.

He was a follower of Gandhi, a committed pacifist. He could understand hating Hitler, but he drew the line at loving England. The sudden gung-ho jingoism of his Indian brothers in arms he found incomprehensible. He was a lonely and ill-tempered figure now.

I was just tired and hungry all the time. Meals in the canteen in the Waldorf were still okay, although nothing like they had been in pre-war days, but making our rations into something resembling an appetising meal was so far beyond my meagre cooking skills, it wasn't funny. So when he was home we mostly ate out, often having to abandon a half-eaten meal when the sirens wailed. And how they wailed. Night after night after night; you could set your clocks by them.

After two months we were really ragged. Rikh couldn't understand why I "deliberately" put us in danger, refusing to swop London for the safe haven of the country. I tried to humour him while refusing to give ground, but he was far too clever to fall for that. He knew me very well and, although he didn't know what was going on, he knew something was. My "carry on regardless" attitude may have been appropriate as a practical means for enduring a war, but it was a lousy means of conducting a relationship. "Make do and mend."

It was no substitute for love. Rikh was being short-changed and somewhere he knew it.

Mother and I continued to meet on Thursdays as before. But now we parted earlier to try and get home before the bombs started falling. It seems strange to me now that we didn't stay together, but scurried away to our separate burrows, like frightened animals.

What was really peculiar was that when we had timed it wrong, and I was rushing to get home in the midst of an air raid, sometimes there was still a bus running. It was rare, but it did happen. Transport in those days was at the driver's discretion, so if he thought his route was clear, he carried on. It was a wonderful and cheering sight, running past falling buildings, swept off your feet by blast, in a shower of broken glass and soaking wet from a burst water main, choking in the dust, to see a dear old red bus come chugging out of the fug, determined to make its way home.

How did we stand it? I don't know. By and large, we weren't brave. We weren't heroes. We just carried on. We endured. Perhaps that's what courage is, after all? It didn't feel like it. I was scared most of the time. Especially when the bombs were falling all around. What terrified me most was the prospect of being buried alive, trapped beneath the rubble, injured and alone.

Then I would curse my stubborn stupidity and vow I would get myself to Welwyn at the crack of dawn the next day, or as soon as the trains were running again, but in the end the long night would pass and in the morning I just turned my back on my fears and got on with it. We all did.

I was unfaithful to Rikh long before we left England.

The War seemed to have heightened everyone's emotions except his. When you wake up in the morning and think you may be dead by teatime, it changes everything. A new and powerful perspective took over, a determination to do what I wanted with my life while I still had it. I often wondered what the hell I was doing, but never enough to stop me. There was no time to reflect, still less to regret.

It was not that I didn't love Rikh. I did, very much, and I revered his intelligence and judgement, but, at the end of the day, that was the problem, it was all so cerebral. I had longed for a great love, a soulmate, and what I had was a judge and jury. A mentor, not a friend. Rikh had vision: he was a kind and compassionate man when not irritated by the pygmies that surrounded him. But I seemed to have become one of them in his eyes and that was not a comfort when the world was falling down around our ears. Maybe, in the end, Yolanda was right. At the beginning, she had said he was a "dry stick" and he was. Also the difference in our ages, which at first had leant our liaison such glamour, began to tell.

With the prospect of death daily I began to want my life—my youth—some rapture while I was still capable of it. Lal had taught me what passion was and I wanted more. I found that I loved sex. I needed it and wanted it and Rikh did not. He didn't really like sex at all. Or so it seemed to me. It was all far too unpredictable for him; a wild, careless joy ride whose outcome he could not foresee. I always had the feeling when we made love that a part of him remained aloof, averted, turned away almost as if in distaste. Whatever it was, it didn't make for great sex. And I was still young enough to long for moons in June and a headlong passion, come desolation or delight.

So the long nights, when London was shrouded in darkness and the bombing created such disruption that transport became utter chaos, provided the perfect cover for any brief liaison. I was not the only one. It was going on all around me.

I would meet a perfect stranger, often in the pub in Maddox Street, for a few intoxicating hours and then they were gone. London in those days was full of men passing through. Young men who might be dead, wounded or maimed in a week's time. Boys who wanted to squeeze some joy out of life while they still could. Our motto was "live for today, for tomorrow may never come." It didn't for so many.

I had a lot of these encounters. Most of them boys, very

few were over twenty-one, who were rather sweet. They were all oddly sentimental, fiercely physical, a bit sheepish afterwards, almost apologetic. I didn't mind at all. I didn't want tenderness, I wanted passion. So mostly we went for a drink, talked for an alarmingly short time and then the comforting oblivion of sex with a stranger. Selfish, no questions asked. Brief, heady bliss. Mostly in the cheap hotels that abounded in London in those days, often near the great railway termini, with stained carpets and mismatched sheets. We didn't care. We weren't there for the décor.

Once, shamefully, even up against a wall in a dark alley, just off St Martin's Lane, during an air raid while the bombs rained down around us. A desperate need, born of fear, satisfied and then over. Just like dogs. No strings. We hardly even looked at each other when it was over. Just went our separate ways. Neither knowing nor caring what became of the other. That was the worst of my excesses. I can't even remember his name. I'm not sure I ever knew.

Afterwards, what worried me most was that I liked it that way. Death was so random in those days. The raids were relentless—night after night, every night. They became the only thing we could rely on. Although we claimed to be "carrying on," "business as usual." It was actually anything piped but, whistling in the dark was more like it. The whole fabric of our lives was being torn apart. Journeys across London that had taken minutes now took hours, as we had to negotiate blocked roads and burst water mains, gas and sewer pipes. And everywhere the sweet smell of escaping gas and what we later learned was dead bodies. And the dust, mountains of it rising from canyons of rubble where whole streets had been. Shopping for food now took forever—queuing endlessly after a day's work. The staples like butter, meat, eggs, and sugar—previously taken for granted, now were rare treats.

"We can take it" was our proud boast. But could we? I began to doubt it frankly as the bombing went on and on and the most basic normal activities—getting to work, washing, obtaining food—became increasingly difficult. And with the madness born of never enough sleep and a constant sore throat from inhaling dust and burnt matter, normal life ceased to exist.

Somehow though we did carry on, after a fashion, and to our eternal credit we didn't cave in like the rest of Europe, but it seems to me, looking back from the serene oasis of decades of peace, that we were all a bit mad in those days. Certainly I was. How could we avoid it? Life had become a jittery dance macabre. The daily euphoria of cheating death. We all became fatalists. "What will be will be." We learned not to care about consequences. It was so unlikely there would ever be any.

For Rikh and I our romance—our first feverish longing to be together and delight in the two damp rooms that we called home—had long petered out, swept away by a tidal wave of the ordinary. It is hard to remain in love with your

Romeo when his noble head is framed by a backdrop of drying socks and dripping underwear.

I kept my growing disillusionment and secret liaisons tightly to myself until one evening when Yolanda and I waited after work for a bus that never came. Rikh was away on ops and would not be back for weeks, if at all, and Derek was working all hours at his hospital. So we gave up and took refuge in the nearest pub. We drank too many Sherries and shared a packet of crisps and I blurted it all out to her. The whole thing. I hadn't meant to. I told her everything, how I felt about Rikh, how I still longed for Lal, my liberating fumbles in the dark. I regretted it instantly. She had such a firm moral compass. She was bound to hate me.

She didn't. She looked at me impassively for a moment, then nodded.

"I know. Relationships are hell."

I laughed. I was too shocked to do anything else and too immature and self-centred to wonder what iceberg of despair lay beneath that bleakness.

What had gone wrong? I had thought she was still happy with Derek. How had he hurt her so much that she felt like that? I'm ashamed to say I never knew. I was so caught up with myself, I didn't ask. I reverted to type, focused only on myself and ignored anything else. I was not a good friend to her then. God knows, she deserved better.

Now, after all is said and done, as an old woman it is that

shame that stays with me. That wakes me in the night and fills me with regret. Sometimes even tears. My failure to care for her as she cared for me shames me far more than the memory of any random coupling in the dark.

Yolanda never spoke like that again. She continued to share her life with Derek—of that I was certain—she spoke of him constantly, but the bloom had died. Whatever joy he'd caused her to feel had gone.

We saw a lot of each other during this period. We were "grass widows" after all, and we worked together. Rikh was away most of the time and Derek was on duty at the hospital round the clock. He hardly ever came home, Yolanda said. So she and I would snatch a quick supper together most nights in town before the trek north, she to her first aid post, me to my fire watching on the roof.

Mostly it was the ABC or Joe Lyons in the Strand, but once in a while we pushed the boat out. A friend or business associate of the Barronis would offer us a delicious meal. As enemy aliens, Italians in London were doing very badly. Papa B could no longer import his goods from Italy and was now living in semi-retirement. He and Mama B kept a low profile these days. Carlo hardly dared go out any more. Friends of theirs had had bricks thrown through their windows and abuse yelled at them in the street. Yolanda was particularly concerned about her elder brother, Vittorio. He had been born in Italy. She and Carlo were all right. They were born in London and Papa B had had the foresight to make sure they were British citizens.

But Mama, Papa and Vittorio were not and as enemy aliens they could be rounded up and interned. Many were. Some were even sent to Canada. For some reason Mama and Papa B seemed to regard that as the worse fate of all. They moaned and wailed until Y, exasperated, pointed out that they could be sent back to Italy and with her political affiliations, anyone in her family would become "Musso's punchbag," as she put it. They shut up after that. But they had to report to the local police station once a week like criminals. They were anxious and afraid and I hated to see them like that.

One night Yolanda and I went to a little restaurant in Soho run by a cousin of her mother's. Nobody much was there and we had the place to ourselves. We ate lovely spaghetti puttanesca and drank a special bottle of wine given us by the proprietor, Paolo. As he poured the wine, he told us that the restaurant was now almost always empty, that his friends and neighbours shunned him, he had been shouted at in the street and his son beaten up on the way home. He said that he had lived and worked in Soho for forty years, "before this world war" and now suddenly he was an "enemy" and an "alien". We commiserated with him, sat long over our meal and lost track of time.

At one point I ventured that I thought perhaps we should start spending some evenings with Y's parents. I hated the thought that they might feel ostracised.

"No need," she replied succinctly.

"Why not?"

"Pipped to the post. They already have a regular dinner guest. One who brings them all sorts of goodies from the day job."

I smiled, relieved that they were being supported.

"Every week. Without fail. Fridays, I think."

"Ah," I said knowingly, "Next door or Uncle Vittorio?" They had lovely neighbours. The Bernsteins—an elderly Jewish couple of Austrian extraction who were probably going through something similar themselves.

"Neither, as it happens. A lady. An English lady."

I should have known. Mother. I felt incredibly proud of her at that moment. "For God's sake, don't let her catch you calling her English."

We laughed and then I had to go to the Ladies. When I came back she looked at me seriously and said,

"I've got something to tell you." She lit a cigarette and inhaled deeply.

"I'm pregnant."

"What does Derek think?"

"Nothing. He doesn't know." So it wasn't all right at all. She grinned, forcing a cheerfulness she did not feel. "You... you are my sole confidante."

"Do you want a child?"

"Oddly enough, yes. Not sure I want a husband though."

"Don't you mind that...?"

"No. Not at all. You turned out all right, didn't you?"

She smiled at my anxious face. I was being torn in so many directions. Concern for her and her child, overwhelming sympathy for another bastard offspring, knowledge of what that meant. We had thrown aside convention, but I doubted the rest of the world had. I knew exactly what was in store for both of them. Yolanda was going to need all the courage she possessed to go through with this. My face said as much.

"Can't say I'm looking forward to telling Mama and Papa though. Especially Papa. Mama will howl and wail, but she'll come round. Papa? I don't know. Catholic fathers... they really believe all that stuff." For once she looked a bit daunted.

"Then don't do it alone. I'll come with you. *Contra mundem*. Remember?" She smiled her lop-sided smile and raised her glass.

"To you, cara." We drank. I raised mine.

"To us. Whatever the future brings."

We wound up the evening on that note; thanking Paolo for the wine and the delicious food he had charged us so little for, then paying the bill and saying a hurried goodbye, she going off to her bus and I to mine as the sirens began to wail.

I made it home that night. She did not.

I attended her funeral at the Italian church in Clerkenwell a few days later. Mother and Rikh both offered to accompany me, but I refused. I wanted to go alone. I had been alone when I first met Yolanda, more alone than at any other time in my life and I wanted to be alone now.

Her brothers wept noisily throughout the service, but her parents were silent, suddenly old, bowed with sorrow. I watched them walk slowly down the aisle, dressed in unrelieved black, bearing a grief beyond tears. They had asked me to sit with them but I had said no. As gently as I could. I knew that I would not be able to comfort them and it would be unthinkable to allow them to comfort me. I knew they would try.

Besides, we were not family, Yolanda and I. The bond we had was deeper than blood; it was one of choice, of sympathy and understanding. The random instinct of love.

I sat at the back of the church, half-hidden by a pillar. Where I could remember her on my own. The girl with a name as daft as mine.

I didn't go to the burial. I couldn't bear to see her put into the ground.

I saw Derek, his face rigid with grief, walk out of the church with her family and knew I could never see him again. She had chosen me to keep her secret and I would never betray her trust now.

Chapter Fifteen

I hung on at the Waldorf for a few months after Yolanda's death. Feeling like a stray dog. There were many of those in London at that time, mangy, starving wretches, cowering and bereft, clinging to the ruins of their old homes, unable to understand why they were suddenly alone.

The raids went on and with them the unthinking routine, stumbled through with increasing exhaustion. I have a mental image of myself at that time running: running everywhere, from work to home to shelter, never at rest, fleeing from bombs, fleeing from death, fleeing from grief.

Then spring came and the sudden sunlight and resurgence of life seemed a terrible parody. All life was around me, but she was not there to see it. The tender leaves, the nascent buds, the flowering weeds that grew in profusion on the bomb sites, all seemed cruel, taunting.

London with its wanton resilience and death on every street corner became hateful to me. Its dear familiarity mocked my grief.

I left London that summer. One bright sunny afternoon I walked out of the Waldorf and I never went back. I took the coward's way out and wrote a letter of resignation to the GM, claiming my husband had been transferred and I had to go with him. That night I told Rikh I would live with him in Welwyn Garden City. Within a week we left London. There wasn't much to move.

I wanted out—to be in a place, any place, untainted by memory. So I buried myself in that dreary dormitory town where everything was pleasant and nothing remarkable, where every house and every life was the same. There I played at being a housewife. I even learned to make bread—to Rikh's delight.

I busied myself for every waking hour. I cooked and cleaned and polished, I sewed and knitted with the WVS—I who had prided myself on smashing convention. I wanted another life, one as different from mine as possible. I was in freefall. I realise now that Yolanda had been not only my best friend and confidante, she had been my point of reference in all things; the beacon from which I could find my bearings. Without her I did not know who I was, or how to be.

I knew I should see the Barronis before I left, but I am ashamed to say I never did. I never saw them again after the funeral. That day was burned into my brain, and what grew back was only scar tissue, numb and dumb, incapable of feeling. Our grief stretched out between us like a chasm we could not cross. She had brought us together and her death had torn us apart.

Mother continued to see them. And me. As we no longer met in town, on her day off, every week, she doggedly made the journey to me by train, braving raids and endlessly disrupted travel. She used to come on a Monday to help me with the washing. It took her eight hours to get home on one occasion. They had bombed the railway line and the tracks had buckled; so the train stopped further up the line and all the passengers had to get off and walk along the siding to the nearest station, then make their way home on whatever buses were still running.

She came back as usual the following week. Nothing daunted her. But then she was not a coward and I was.

As the relentless boredom of the suburbs began to pall, even in my dulled state, I began to flirt. I was a great hit in the Officers' Mess. Women were at a premium on an air force base and the WAAFs weren't much competition. How could they be with their bulky uniforms and lace up shoes? I was not bad looking in those days and I was drawn to men like a moth to a flame. I could see the admiration in their eyes.

So I emerged from my self-imposed purdah. I unpacked my clothes from the case, where they had stayed untouched for months, and washed and ironed them.

Then I put on my best dress and my war paint and went on the prowl. A magpie among sparrows. Looking for someone else's eggs. It wasn't difficult. Young men were all the same. Or so it seemed to me. I soon resumed my old bad habits. You can't teach an old bitch new tricks. But it was foolish and rotten of me to play them out on Rikh's home turf.

I didn't care. I didn't care about anything much then. Least of all my transient partners. We used each other and moved on. That was all there was to it. Or so I told myself. A kiss and cuddle in the dark, a long drive into the country when Rikh was flying ops, the easy bliss of love with a stranger. If you can call it love.

Rikh didn't seem to notice. As long as I preserved appearances while he was there, he didn't really seem to mind what I got up to when his back was turned. Or if he did, he never said. And I kept everything secret, or so I thought. But there were those who knew—those with sharp eyes and no lives of their own, with time to spare for the vicarious thrill of spying on others. The officers' wives, faded and flowery, jealous of my youth and looks. My desperate need to take risks.

They didn't keep their suspicions to themselves. One day, as I left the base library, a new clutch of unread books in my basket, carried for me by a very sweet young Flight Lieutenant, Rikh's Commanding Officer took me aside. His voice crisp with dislike, he said, "Mrs Rikh, what you get up to is your affair. That's between you and your unfortunate husband. But the second I hear so much as a whisper of discord between my men because of you, I'll have you run off this station like the cheap little tramp you are. So pull your horns in and behave, Missy, or you'll be out of here before your feet can touch the ground."

He looked at me with something approaching hate, then turned his back and strode off. He never spoke to me again. He didn't have to. I got the message. Some of the boys I had thought were like me had become smitten. They were still young enough to fall in love. I was disgusted with myself, or rather the self I saw in his eyes. A cruel little bitch who played conquests with children about to die. Who toyed with others' feelings because she had none of her own. Through him, I learned a very basic truth. Grief does not ennoble us: it makes us callous.

And so we lived. From hand to mouth, or so it seemed, certainly in emotional terms. Me, hiding in the hobbled safety of my dormitory town, the garden city. A contradiction in terms if ever there was one. It was for me always a source of wry amusement. A garden city! It said it all. While Rikh and his brothers in arms risked their lives high up in the air, I stayed safely below among those whose main concern was the state of their herbaceous borders. We busied ourselves with a thousand useless tasks, far from the front-line of life, averting our gaze from the slaughterhouse our world had become. The trouble for me in Welwyn was, although I had chosen it, it always felt like exile to me.

But during that winter, that hibernation, the tide of the war slowly began to turn. The Russians, with obscene courage and utter disregard for human life, held onto Stalingrad and began to push back the German army. We had our first victory at El Alamein and that gave a huge lift to our morale. And with America's entry into the war, vast resources of men and arms, food and fuel flooded into our island, and we began to feel a distant whisper of hope, the first faint glimmer of the possibility—at first so tenuous we hardly dared think it—of victory. Germany began to be bombed around the clock. I am ashamed to say that at the time it didn't bother me at all. If I had thought about it, I would have been glad.

In late November Rikh received orders that his squadron was to be posted overseas. He held his breath and prayed for India, that at last the force that had so oppressed his people would return him to them. We waited for three anxious weeks and then a few days before Christmas Eve, Rikh received the present he had been hoping for. His squadron's posting was to Ambala, in Northern India. I came back late one night, sated and drunken, from a hurried encounter with a young boy about to be shipped off to Canada for flight training, and found Rikh sitting in our poky living room in shirt sleeves, his thinning hair awry. I thought at first this is it, I've done it now. Pushed him too far, but he looked up at me, his face radiant as a young bride, his dark eyes full of light and said, "I'm going home." He began to cry. I held him in my arms, ashamed at my indifference to his sorrows, his botched and painful journey. It didn't occur to me to ask if I was going too.

In the following days, our situation became clear. Airmen in the Royal Indian Air Force were being "returned" to train for operations in the East. Very few of them had families in Britain, but those that did could be "returned" with them. Rikh read out the order, then smiled at me beatifically and said "That means you."

So, it was settled. I was going to India at last. If we survived the journey—on a troopship in a convoy across the Atlantic, with attending U-boats, all hell bent on our destruction, through the Panama Canal, then to New Zealand for a month while we waited to join another convoy, then on to Ceylon and Madras. A journey to another world, a voyage to countries I had never imagined I'd ever see. If we survived long enough to see them, that is. The Atlantic was less of a hazard than it had been, but the battle was still far from being won. Convoys were attacked and shipping lost on a regular and plentiful basis.

Rikh began immediately to make his plans for departure. There seemed to be an awful lot of them. Lists were drawn up with the attention and scope of a military campaign. He planned everything down to the smallest detail. Lists of friends to say goodbye to, League business that had been abandoned because of his military service had to be wound up or "properly" handed over, he insisted, and "supplies" had to be bought. It did occur to me that if things in India were so bad that we had to provision ourselves from ration bound, shortage ruled Britain, then we were in for a lean time indeed. But for the first time in years, perhaps ever in my knowledge of him, Rikh was happy. He revelled in his plans and preparations. The sullen silences and gloomy moods of recent months were gone, replaced with a snappy efficiency and cheerfulness that was entirely new. All the things that had so bedevilled him—the short-sightedness and arrogance of his Commanding Officers, the jingoistic silliness of his fellow servicemen, even the cold of winter and the tastelessness of the food—bothered him no more. In fact, almost the reverse, now he knew he was leaving they were already taking on a kind of perverse sepia charm, an Anne Hathaway's cottage view of England. Cosy, quaint, quirky. Memory was taking over from observation and, with it, a tolerance he'd certainly never had before. I laughed at him. Told him he'd be making scones next, and he just laughed and smiled his new sunny smile. He was unrecognisable. It was strange, but rather engaging. We were an odd pair, he and I. Diametrically opposite, drawn together and then pulled apart with equal force. I never really understood what held us together or tore us apart.

He went up to London several times in pursuit of his "preparations". He did ask me to go with him, but I refused. I pretended I was busy with other things and he didn't press me. I knew that when I did go it would be to bid farewell to everything I had ever loved. Mother, my home, the memory of Yolanda in every dear, familiar place, the possibility of ever seeing Lal again. I dreaded even the idea of it. I had left London by choice, but my flight had only been partial. Hedging my bets in Welwyn, I had run away to a place I could easily return from. That would no longer be the case. I was going halfway round the world this time and a world that was at war. Who knew when, if ever, I would be back? And what would remain if I did.

Rikh had acquired a rather battered shipping trunk and put most of our books in it. I kept out my school prize, a rather lovely illustrated Omar Khayyam and Yolanda's book of John Donne poems, borrowed by me and never returned, her favourite. These I would keep with me.

Rikh then began to go through our clothes. One evening while we were eating supper, a meal he was polite about, but did not actually eat due to the absence of chillies, he said gently, "I think you will have to go to London one day soon." I felt sick.

"I know." I mumbled. "This cottage pie isn't too bad, is it?" It was awful and we both knew it from the way we pushed it about our plates rather than eat it.

He handed me a generous wad of notes. "Buy yourself some clothes."

I did need it. My everyday stuff dated back to the early days at the Waldorf and the black costume was beginning to show its age. I took the money.

"Get another suit. They're always useful. But serviceable, navy or grey. Medium weight. Warm enough under an overcoat in the Atlantic, cool enough with a blouse in India."

I nodded, but I wasn't really listening. I was too busy dreading my return to London. Rikh gave me a list of things he thought I ought to buy and I arranged to meet Mother in the Cumberland, when the ordeal would be nearly over.

Mother changed the arrangements at the last minute. She sent me a telegram. She'd never done that before. For a moment I felt giddy, wondering what was in it. But only a cryptic line. "Change of plan. Meet by Round Pond. Same time. Mother." No more. She never was much of a one for explaining herself.

Chapter Sixteen

I took the train down to London on a quiet day between Christmas and New Year. The train was unheated and almost empty, wiser souls staying at home, and I shivered in the carriage. Whether from dread or cold I don't know. A kind soldier offered me his great coat as a rug. But I declined. It was sweet of him and he looked like a nice lad, fresh-faced and smiling, but I didn't want any complications of that sort. Not this time. So I discouraged his attempts to strike up a conversation and stared resolutely out of the window. The journey through the frozen landscape seemed to take forever, but at last the train pulled into the great glass cathedral of King's Cross station and I got out and made my way to the bus stop outside.

I took the bus to Oxford Circus. London exuded a tired, listless air. The streets were in ruins, filthy with the dust of a thousand crumbled buildings, and the random detritus of people's lives. From my seat at the top of the bus I saw a house, almost entirely destroyed, with only one wall left standing, but oddly enough, its white marble mantelpiece completely intact, undamaged, even to the framed family photographs that still stood on it.

I got off the bus and picked my way down the broad sweep of Regent's Street, formerly so elegant, past huge craters where the smart shops and restaurants had been. The pavement beneath my feet was coated with a residue of grit and broken glass, and I scrunched my way along, feeling as if I was shattering the past with every step. I saw the massive broken masonry of Regency London and wondered who was buried beneath it.

I tried to look in the windows of the shops that remained, but my heart wasn't in it. Those that were open had boarded windows and advertised 'Bomb Damage Stock'. It was profoundly disheartening. I had never shopped for clothes on my own before. As a child I went with Mother and since school days always with Yolanda. I thought of our window shopping sprees and the fun we had, laughing and staring in amazement at the window displays. We used to spend hours trying on clothes we could never afford and always consoled ourselves with a hearty lunch or supper afterwards.

Now I walked on alone, my longing for her so intense that I could hardly breathe. I walked on past the landscape of our youth, and felt as desolate as my surroundings. I wondered if Derek missed her as much as I did; I hated to think how Mama B must feel.

I walked past the fountain where Eros used to be (even he wasn't there anymore) and into the first shop in Piccadilly. As soon as I was inside, I realised my mistake. It was far too grand for me. It was one of those places that called themselves "exclusive"—all plush carpet, gilt chairs and so-called Paris fashions. With appropriate price tags and only one model of each. I sighed: I should have gone to Swan and Edgar.

A cheery looking girl came up and asked if she could help me. Only if you can raise the dead, I thought. She ventured brightly could she make a suggestion? I felt too dispirited to argue. So I launched into a lack lustre recitation of Rikh's list of requirements. Serviceable, two piece, medium weight, navy or grey.

Her face fell. I explained it was wanted for a voyage, so it must be practical, hard-wearing and versatile. She asked me where I was going. I hedged a bit, but she persisted. She was an odd one. She didn't look like she belonged in that shop. She was far too friendly. Despite her smart dress, she lacked the obligatory look of disdain and the fake French accent the 'modistes' always seem to have in such establishments.

I found that I ended up telling her far more than I had intended, or probably should have. But she was so chatty and warm, so genuine; not good-looking, too short and broad in the beam for that, but she had lovely bright blue eyes and a mischievous grin. I kind of warmed to her without really knowing why.

Then she said I should never wear grey. Frankly, I thought that was a damn cheek and I must have looked a bit askance because she quickly said that she had two suits in mind. Both absolutely beautiful. One a deep claret red and the other a sort of soft mid green. She showed them to me and she was right. They were so elegant, so beautifully cut that they could have been Paris models. Wearily, I told her they were out of my league. She said "Try 'em on. You don't have to buy 'em."

I hesitated. "Go on," she urged, "for a giggle." And I thought oh hell why not? So I did.

I tried the red first. When I walked out of the changing room, she beamed and told me I looked like a film star. A million dollars, I think she said. Then the older lady, who was clearly the manageress, and who did have the fake French accent, came up and cooed over me as if I were her new born babe. She didn't need to. One glance in the mirror told me I'd never looked better in my life. I blanched a bit when I saw the price tag though. It was hefty, but not impossible. But it would mean that if I bought it, I would have nothing left over for anything else; no new stockings or unmentionables. I stared at my reflection, looking for the answer. Then a laughing voice came back to me. "One day we'll dress you in scarlet." That did it. I would travel to a new world and a new life, clad in the colours of the girl who had made me dare.

I told the shop assistant I'd take it. She grabbed it off me and ran to the cash desk, as if scared I'd change my mind. Halfway there, she turned and muttered out of the corner of her mouth, "you'll never regret it." Then she nodded towards the manageress and rolled her eyes. As I was waiting to pay the manageress, who looked like a real hard old piece with her blood red lips and her painted on eyebrows, snapped and snarled at her and grinned and grovelled at me. I twigged. So I played along, chatting apparently at random, saying what a gem the girl was, that I would never have chosen it without her, and I was utterly delighted.

The Old Bat pursued her lips. The girl winked at me. I hoped she got a commission, but I doubt it. In the end I paid and left the shop. I think we all thought each other insane. But she was very nice, or perhaps she just wanted a sale. Oddly though, it did cheer me up. I left the shop feeling much better than I had when I entered it. And the suit was lovely. I wore it for years. It had a kind of timeless elegance. And the colour was gorgeous. Deep and vivid, the colour of good wine. Yolanda would have loved it. And that gave me huge comfort.

I met Mother as she had requested by the Round Pond in Kensington Gardens. It was a cold dark afternoon, the sky overcast, the wind icy. An odd choice for our meeting, but not such an odd place. A place full of memory. A stone's throw from Peel Street.

I showed her my suit while it was still light. She smiled. "Very adventurous, Jeannie."

"Do you think it's too much?"

"No, I don't. It's a bold, definite statement. Ideal for a journey." We fell silent after that.

After a bit, she got up. "We should keep moving. It's too cold to sit still."

The Gardens were beginning to empty. Only the most Spartan had braved the cold and wind. A few starched, uniformed nannies scurried away, taking their bundled up charges home to tea. We walked on down the path to the statue of Peter Pan.

Memory was beginning to take over; she had brought me here so often in the past. Usually when we were trying to keep out of Cornelius' way. I tried to take her hand. She wouldn't have it. As always, she squeezed mine briefly and then let go.

"I used to come and sit here for hours. Before you were born. I like the gardens better in winter."

She was almost talking to herself. The harsh wind blew, bringing the blood to our cheeks.

"I'd wonder what on earth I should do. And I'd sit and look at him and wish he could whisk me away to Neverland."

She laughed, but it was a bitter, rueful sound, as if it hurt her throat

"I still had hopes of going home then. I felt sick all the time, my clothes didn't fit and I was young enough to want my mother." She looked down, screwed up her mouth. "Then Duncan died..." she swallowed hard, "and after that I knew there was no going back." She looked across at me and said defiantly.

"You were a beautiful baby. You won a church competition once, Most Beautiful Baby, did I ever tell you that?"

No, she had not. "Well, Jeannie, we had better get out of this cold." She headed purposefully for the exit, setting a brisk pace. I hurried after her.

"Do you ever think of them?"

"Who?"

"Your family?"

She faltered, then bit her lip.

"Oh yes. All the time."

She walked on. I stood stock still, grieving for the child that was my mother and the bleakness of the life I had condemned her to. She came back and touched my face with her gloved hand.

"Stop that now. It's a hard lesson, Jeannie. Some things stay broken. That's all. I was always sad, but never sorry." She smiled her bright courageous smile that was full of pain and walked on.

Years later, a world apart in time and place, a postcard arrived for me, unsigned. A black and white photograph of the statue of Peter Pan. On the back was written, "Do you remember?"

I did. I still do.

Rikh was not impressed by my new suit and even less by the fact that it had cost so much that I had had to forego all other sundries. I put it on for him when I got home. All he said was, "Joined the fire service?"

He went back to reading his paper. I felt as if a bucket of cold water had just been thrown over me.

"It's not so red." On the back foot already.

"Oh, it's a lovely colour, but it's not what you'd call serviceable is it?"

I couldn't answer him. I had felt brave and beautiful, now I just felt stupid. Defensive and guilty like a naughty child. And it occurred to me as I stood in that cramped suburban kitchen, pleading for approval from a man who would not even look at me, that that's what I would always be in his eyes. I even wondered how much of my delinquent behaviour was due to his oppressive quasi-fatherhood. Glimmers of understanding were beginning to pierce the dark corners of my life. It would never look the same again.

We took the train from Euston to Liverpool a few days later. Mother came to the station. She held me tight, then pushed me away. "You stay safe," she said sternly. As if my survival was only a matter of good behaviour and entirely within my control, like using your hankie or washing behind your ears.

Then she smiled grimly at Rikh and left. She did not stay to wave. I didn't mind. We had already said our goodbyes.

We shoved our way through the crowds. The station was heaving with soldiers, sailors, airmen, laughing girls putting on a brave face and silent, sorrowing parents, all saying goodbye. Special trains had been earmarked for the convoys and our tickets were checked thoroughly to make sure we got on the right train.

Outside, it was getting dark. London in the late afternoon of winter. A time for home, slippers and the radio show, a bite of supper. All across the city people were streaming home from work. But not us. That London was no longer for us any more. Before we left, it was already past.

The service men shouted and swore as we pushed past them down the platform, kissed their girls or mothers goodbye, a determinedly brave smile on their lips. Cheerful talk; a swaggering male bravado. Clad in stiff new uniforms, festooned in the paraphernalia of war, I was struck by their youthfulness—their fresh young faces, barely shaved, some still spotty, the carefully brillianteened hair, all jaunty, joking, pretending. Lads out for a laugh.

Now I could weep for them and of the faces I can remember—one in particular comes to mind, a lad with bright red hair, a fixed anxious grin, still chubby face, big splodgy freckles that ran into each other. He winked at me, giving me what Freddy called "the glad eye." Now I wonder what happened to that boy and if he made it. We would not know each other now if we walked past the other in the street, slow and clumsy with age, raddled with aches and pains and bad temper. Or was he killed when he was still a child, cheated of his manhood? I think of him sometimes. God knows why. For some reason or other, his face has stuck in my mind. I hope he made it.

There were groups of children too—evacuees on their way to safe haven in Canada. They were mostly quiet, wide-eyed, all with cardboard boxes on a string round their necks, carrying their gas masks, labels tied to their coats, little human parcels. They seemed far too young to be going so far away.

We pushed and jostled our way into the crowded compartment, found our seats and fought for space in the rack above for the myriad of small bags and boxes Rikh had declared he could not travel without. He was terribly fussy about such things. We smiled at our fellow passengers, all of us crammed in together, elbow to elbow, knee to knee, in horrible proximity, some grumbling, some evincing a good will I am pretty certain they did not feel. After much whistle blowing and false starts, the train shunted back and forth, then stopped. We waited for ages. We had still not left the platform, only progressed a few feet down it. I muttered to Rikh, "If we carry on like this, we'll be dead of old age before we get to India." He just pulled a face, but a young airman, with bright blue eyes and a prematurely lined face, sitting opposite smiled at me, and said "we should be so lucky." He seemed nice, so I smiled back and nodded. If Rikh was going to take refuge in a sullen silence, at least there would be someone to talk to.

Then at last, we were on our way. The train was painfully slow. The corridors were packed with troops, sitting on the floor, smoking and playing cards. Getting to the loo involved a perilous clambering over numerous men, all whistling and trying to grab whatever bit of me was nearest to them. When I reached the loo, two airmen were already asleep, curled upon the floor, having been copiously sick in the bowl. I decided not to bother, but wondered how on earth we would all manage. Liverpool is a long way from London.

It took forever. Packed like sardines, we slept sitting up, heads lolling on strangers' shoulders. It was also freezing, the train was unheated. In the country now, the darkness outside seemed impenetrable, almost solid. A black blanket of night. Inside the compartment, the blackout lamps cast an eerie blue light on the faces beneath, turning them into masks, stern and immobile, barely human. We look like ghouls in a horror film, I thought. At some point it started to snow, thin white flakes beat against the windows, forming icy margins round the frames. I had no idea where we were or how long we'd been travelling. My arm was so closely packed into my sleeping neighbour's side, I didn't dare raise it to look at my watch, I would certainly have woken him. I dozed fitfully, waking at intervals and envying those who had slept soundly since we left Euston.

Then we were all woken up by a crash and the high-pitched squeal of protesting brakes. The train juddered to a halt. Then the lights went out. I grabbed Rikh's hand. At least I hoped it was his. I couldn't tell in that darkness. The airman lit a match. Its fleeting light showed me it was Rikh's hand. I sighed with relief and let go. The airman passed me a cigarette and I was grateful for it. We sat and waited for the shrill whistle of falling bombs.

Nothing happened. We sat in silence, smoking. After what seemed like hours a shout was heard, "Unexploded bomb on the line." Probably the conductor, at any rate whoever he was, he sounded terribly unconcerned. I suppose it was an everyday occurrence for him. We all began to breathe again.

We waited. Still no-one spoke. The pitch black only relieved by the glowing spark of a cigarette. We chain-smoked. There was nothing else to do; and it did soothe your nerves. We could do without everything except nicotine in those days.

After a while, the lights came back on. And, with them, speech. Suddenly everyone was talking at once. With the advent of light we were no longer sitting ducks, cowering in the dark, fearful of each tiny sound. We stretched and yawned, shuffling in our confined spaces and began to exchange platitudes. "Crikey, I thought we'd had it when the bleedin' lights went out," "God, it's cold in here" (that was me), "Yeah. Brass monkey weather innit, luv?"

Sandwiches were brought out, made with awful

National flour bread, "wheatmeal" it was called, nothing wheaty about it at all, it was pale grey and tasted of cardboard, filled with spam, which believe it or not was a treat then, or a scrape of marrow jam. Rikh had made ours and he had used up the last tin of spam and about half a tin of mustard powder, so at least they tasted of something. They made your eyes water, those sandwiches, but we shared them out and they were very popular. We drank stewed tea from our Thermoses and a bottle of pale ale was passed round. Then we did what the British are masters at. We shut up and made do.

Much later, I went on another expedition to find a functioning toilet. It was right at the other end of the train. The others on the way were worse than the first. At last I found one, but only after trampling on most of the British army, it seemed to me, all yelling lewd suggestions. "A blanket of men, sweetheart, all waiting for you!" and "You can walk on me, darling, any time!"

A young sailor who looked about twelve, evicted the sleeping occupants and guarded the door for me. The lock was broken. He was rather a gentleman, that child, he actually blushed when I asked him to let me through. I was desperate by this time.

He told me the train was so packed there were ten men sleeping in the guards' van. I battled my way back to our compartment, squeezed into my seat and fell asleep.

When I woke it was a cold, grey dawn and we were pulling into Liverpool. An icy rain was falling. Thin arrows of sleet fell into the steely waters of the Mersey; it looked like molten metal. Everything was grey. England in January, I thought, a good time to leave.

Chapter Seventeen

We stumbled off the train, cramped and aching, shivering in the cold dawn air. A rather cross air force liaison officer herded us onto a bus and we were driven off to our billet. It was all getting terribly military. I noticed that although there were quite a few "returned" officers on the bus, some of whom were known to Rikh, there were only a few wives, all English, and no Indian wives at all. I assumed they must all have been left behind in India when the men first came to Britain. Anyway, there were only a few other women who didn't seem at all keen to befriend me. I didn't care. I was going to India. That was all that mattered.

We stayed for two nights in Liverpool. Put up in the Spartan splendour of a boys prep school somewhere on the outskirts of town. I never knew where. All the signposts had been taken down. It was a very odd place—no attempt whatsoever had been made to make a small child feel at home. Bare boards on the floors, battered iron bedsteads with threadbare blankets, rough and scratchy, communal showers and stinking toilets. Yet it was an odd juxtaposition of private squalor and public splendour because, although the dorms and bathrooms were of a kind rarely seen outside a slum, the public rooms—the main hall, class rooms and library—were glorious: all old oak panelling, ornate cornice work and marble fireplaces. The library was vast with its stained glass windows and endless rows of books. A temple to learning in which the incumbents were expected to live an otherwise hard and monastic life. As you left the masters' drawing room, with its leather club armchairs and antique tables with crystal decanters and yellowing magazines and walked along the corridor to the dorms, the walls were lined with children's paintings. Almost all of them were roseate visions of home: smiling Mamas, broad and capable, with corkscrew curls, gardens with bright flowers in full bloom. Even a cottage with pink roses round the door. It was always summer at home, it seemed. There was even a bustling street scene of London with a bright red bus. But however different the pictures, all were bathed in the golden light of memory and redolent with loss and longing. It seemed to me all wrong. None of the artists could have been older than twelve. The youngest seven, one of the wives told me that with a cheerful callousness that made me shudder. I was never very comfortable in the face of childhood misery. I had far too clear a memory of my own.

War Changes Everything

All I can say about Liverpool—our gateway to the free world, as it was called at the time, certainly it was our lifeline to America—is that I don't know how anyone survived there. They had been bombed around the clock for months on end. If anything, it was even worse than London. The docks had been targeted obviously, and the burnt out hulks of great ships had been towed down the Mersey so as not to obstruct the entry to the harbour. The whole ruined city was lit up by great torches of flame. Billowing black smoke made it dark even in the few daylight hours January afforded. Everywhere the choking smell of burning—it was an absolute hell on earth. Cascades of bombs fell, fires burned all around and always the deafening din of the ack-ack guns that never seemed to stop firing. Both Rikh and I watched the burning city from the comparative safety of the prep school and wondered how we would ever get out of the docks, let alone make it across the Atlantic. Liverpool was no longer a city: it was a battle zone.

But we were lucky, we did get through, and, as we left, there was a ray of hope. Despite the bombing, the ships kept coming in: huge convoys bearing hordes of men, and incredible quantities of food, fuel and weapons pouring into the ruined city. The infinite largesse of the New World. Much of it was destroyed at sea and on shore, but still it kept flowing in, in never-ending waves.

We left Liverpool with great relief. It felt like the front line, but as we boarded our ship and watched this seemingly limitless profusion being disgorged onto the quayside, Rikh said quietly, "How did they ever think they could win against this?" Indeed. Roosevelt's sleeping giant was not only awake, but on the march. The world would never be the same again.

We boarded The Duchess of Richmond late in the afternoon. I couldn't wait to leave the school with its air of regulated unhappiness, but I might not have been quite so glad had I known that the Duchess of Richmond, a converted pre-war liner, was known as the "drunken duchess" because she rolled so much in heavy seas. She had been converted into a troopship, but there were also a few paying passengers. Two wealthy Jewish families who had somehow managed to buy their way out of occupied Europe, fleeing from the hell their home had become.

I liked them very much. Cosmopolitan and cultured, they spoke stilted but painstaking English and had a kind of old fashioned courtesy that was very attractive after the staccato rudeness of the officers' wives. They made no bones about how they felt about us. One bitch even asked me how I would feel about any offspring Rikh and I might have, "black and white pups" she called them. I laughed as I always did when cornered. Rikh stared sternly at her and said not to let them upset me. There would be a lot more of that in India, he warned. The Officers' clubs in India are not London, he commented darkly, they are a bigot's paradise. With hot and cold running servants but only of the native kind. I would have to be prepared for the memsahibs, he said, whose true awfulness knew no bounds. "The female of the species" he quoted, "I always thought Kipling was thinking of the memsahibs when he wrote that." I decided to give them a wide berth.

We were lucky. We had been allotted a small cabin. The men slept on hammocks in what had been the ballroom. I grew fond of the "old Dutch" as the men called her. You could see her former elegance in what had been the palm court (shades of the Waldorf!) and the enormous restaurant with its dais for the band, now a forces canteen. There were times when I was just about the only one there for the officers' sitting. Unlike Rikh, who turned a kind of eau de nil before we had even left harbour, I was a good sailor. Rough seas bothered me not at all. And the Atlantic could get rough in January. The Dutch listed and rolled and most of those aboard kept quietly to themselves and threw up a lot. Not me: I walked twice daily on deck, whatever the weather, kept my eyes firmly fixed on the horizon when I could see it, and was what Rikh called, "disgustingly fit" and quite happy. I made friends with the steward in the dining room, a relic of better times, who was only too delighted to regale me with tales of the Dutch's former glory, while bewailing the terrible standards of the kitchen, now run by the forces catering corps. While I sawed away at leathery grey mutton and dried up mash made with powdered potato, he tantalised me with tales of dainty lobster salads, fillet Tornedos and puddings that were all spun sugar, real ice cream and poached peaches. My mouth watered, my imagination wandered and his lurid descriptions of lovely food made it a lot easier to put down the awful muck we were given. He was a great comfort to me on those lonely evenings in the dining room and we became friends. The officers' wives moaned about the service when they did appear, but at least we were waited on, the men had to queue up at the canteen end and serve themselves.

Rikh kept to his bunk. At first I thought he was laying it on with a trowel, but when the ship pulled out of the harbour, he made the effort to come shakily on deck and stood with me as we slipped away into the night, the landmarks of Liverpool fitfully lit up by the sudden glare of anti-aircraft fire. There were a few of us on deck that night. But not many.

We watched as the waiting escort ships took up their positions around us. Through the blue dusk we could just make out the convoy. A whole armada of ships at anchor. Forty-one in all. Troopships, converted liners like ours, battle cruisers, destroyers, empty cargo ships returning to America. Slowly, ponderously they all took up their positions and we sailed off down the Mersey and out into the open sea.

The 8th January. A new year in a new world. If we made it.

It took us four weeks to cross the Atlantic, zigzagging across the wintry ocean, trying to avoid the U-boats. We had foul weather all the way. Off the coast of Iceland, we endured freezing temperatures, heavy gales, sleet and snow, ploughing through what the Captain called "considerable quantities of field ice." This was particularly scary as we had all been brought up on tales of the Titanic. One glance outside told us that no-one would survive in those waters. The creaking and groaning of the ship was not reassuring. Our fear was further heightened by the fact that this was where our RAF air cover ran out, leaving us with a terrifying six hundred mile gap in the Atlantic before the American Air Force Catalinas could take over.

I remember the vast wintry sky, the rough swell of the sea and the bitter cold. Gales caused icing of the ship: the deck was covered in it and in the heavy wind we had to reduce our speed. One gale reached hurricane force with waves of nearly forty feet. The old Dutch was tossed up and down like a child's toy. The Captain complained that the ship should not have been sent out to cross the Atlantic in such weather, which was not a comfort. We had been used to the destructive power of man, now it was the elements' turn. Its wanton force only emphasized our insignificance.

But what I chiefly remember is the tedium. The weather made us prisoners inside and our days were filled with rules and regulations—when to eat, when to do our washing, lifeboat drills etc. We played cards a lot. Rikh won quite a considerable amount of money from his fellow officers, which didn't make him any more popular. The officers' wives were ghastly, verbally assassinating all who came within their orbit while knitting grey or khaki garments of unspeakable drabness. Madame Lafarges all. I avoided them, and played cards with the Jewish couples who were much more civilised, though never quite free from an undertow of sadness and loss. They had left everything behind: family, home, way of life. Their fate was a wretched one and I found myself fervently wishing them a happier life in the New World. The old one had let them down very badly.

One couple, the Goldmans, became particular friends of mine. She had been a dancer in her youth. When I asked if she had been a ballet dancer, she took a deep drag on her cigarette in the long, jade holder and replied, "No, darling, cabaret," in her heavily accented English. She was a bit racy and a lot of fun. She was still rather glamorous with her bright red lips and chic little hat with the black lace veil. He was a sweetheart and much older than her; you felt it was no love match but rather one of convenience—two waifs and strays clinging together, but she tolerated his rigid Prussian schedule that caused him huge anxiety if broken, and he viewed her rather avant-garde opinions with an amused, fatherly tolerance. He tried to teach me to play chess and he was terribly patient, but I kept forgetting the rules and in the end he had to give up on me. I always sat with them though, they were only glimmer of intelligent company to be had aboard the Duchess of Richmond.

On we ploughed through the filthy weather. On the

rare clear days I remember watching the huge number of ships spread out across the ocean. Our armada—a floating hiatus between sea and sky. I remember being struck by the vastness of it all. It was my first taste of a wider horizon and despite the fear, I found it exhilarating.

Oddly enough the appalling weather, that Rikh proclaimed was killing him with sea sickness (and he was not the only one), probably saved our lives. The rough sea made it hard for the U-boats to surface and, in fact, we saw no enemy action during the voyage, although two ships in the convoy did collide in the fog. Happily, the damage was not serious and they were able to remain with the convoy, although it slowed us down further and at one point all the leader ships had to switch on their navigation lights. That terrified me. Suddenly we were horribly visible. But all in all, we were very lucky. Later we learned that the Allied shipping losses for that month were half what they were in the preceding and following months, due to the atrocious weather.

Then one early evening, we sailed into New York harbour, past the Statue of Liberty. We saw Manhattan's skyline and marvelled at all the lights. After blackout Britain, the light was dazzling. Bright and multi-coloured, flashing and blinking, to our dazed eyes it was like being inside a kaleidoscope. We had an all too brief week there before joining the next convoy going south. New York was sensational. Everything about it was larger than life. The advertisements on the hoardings towered above us—huge, garish, a bit vulgar, even the taxis were bright yellow. Everyone was in a hurry it seemed, eager, thrusting, impatient. There I realised, with some shock, how constrained and shrunken our lives in war-torn Britain had become. They went out and grabbed life with both hands while we had been hiding in holes in the ground, desperate for survival. Here they had everything on a plate. The bars, the restaurants, the nightclubs were buzzing with life, sex and music. The food—unrationed—was rich, varied and in profusion. We ate ourselves into a sort of stupor for the first few days. Hamburgers and ice cream, butter and milk; wine and jam, beautiful fresh fruit; pineapples and peaches—Mother would have loved it. The Golden Door indeed.

I begged Rikh to take me to the Cotton Club. I bargained, cajoled and then screamed at him. To no avail. But luckily the Goldmans wanted to go and they had some family in America. Distant cousins from Minneapolis who had travelled to New York to welcome them. So we all went together. Rikh stayed in our lodgings in a fog of disapproval. I didn't care. We had a wizard time. The music was superb and Heinz Goldman and I danced all night. He may have been old, but his dancing put most young men to shame. We drank weird and wonderful cocktails, flirted with everyone and laughed all the time. It was a fabulous night. It would never have been so much fun if old gruff and grim Rikh had come, although I did tell him all about it just to rub it in, accusing him of becoming a maiden aunt—and chicken to boot.

After too short a stay, we joined another convoy and sailed down the Atlantic seaboard and through the Caribbean, still dodging U-boats, and on through the Panama Canal. From there to New Zealand, where we stayed for a month while waiting for yet another convoy and then, five months after leaving England, we arrived in Madras. India at last.

Chapter Eighteen

We arrived in Madras overnight. I was woken very early by the light. A bright blinding sunlight that streamed in through the porthole. We both dressed hurriedly and rushed up on deck.

The docks were teeming with wall-to-wall humanity. One vast section was entirely military—Army and Air Force personnel, doctors and nurses from the Medical Corps, hundreds, if not thousands, of men and women in uniform, engulfed by their group identity, swarmed down the gangways and onto the docks. Then slowly they began to move apart and gather at their various muster stations, all to disperse in different directions.

Huge grey troop ships, like our own Duchess of Richmond towered above the harbour, battered and dirty but still proudly intact, and, as I stood on deck for the last time, about to leave the iron fortress that had been my home, I felt a strange affection for our scruffy old hulk.

Once so elegant, now so scarred and down at heel, disgorging those she had kept safe in a journey that had taken us across the world, chased by U boats, guarded by destroyers, berthed like a poor relation in the harbours she had once graced with her careless snobbery. She was like us, no longer beautiful and powerful—bruised and bloody but still here.

I walked down the gangway, feeling a bit afraid at leaving my rusty old shell, and as the heat and light of morning hit me I faltered, suddenly giddy, recoiling at this onslaught of the senses. India. At last. The light blazed, the heat was so fierce it felt like walking into a furnace, and everywhere bright colours, a whirling panoply of life.

Beyond the ordered ranks of the military, the whole place was chock full of life. In all its forms: the great and the good, waiting in gold braid, vivid silks and jewels, in chauffeur driven cars, an island of privilege in an ocean of poverty. The scale of which I had never dreamt of let alone seen, the endless ranks of the poor and needy, the beggars and the maimed, all baying for alms, while ragged children hawked their worthless trinkets. I reeled in the face of such tumult.

I missed my footing and stumbled—my first misplaced step on Indian shore. Typically, I had missed what was just in front of me. A small but vociferous demonstration, waving banners—they yelled "Bharat Choro" and "Hindustan Zindabad." I turned to Rikh, who was surveying the scene with an angelic smile. His homecoming could not have been more perfect; he was a man coming into his own. Before I could walk on, a banner was thrust in my face, and a small dark man in a white dhoti with smelly breath and no teeth, yelled "Brits Out!" I looked at him in astonishment.

"Quit India!" he demanded sternly.

I laughed. These were the phrases we had felt so brave chanting in Trafalgar Square and at Speaker's Corner. What we had worked for on cold, rainy evenings in an old Imperial city half a world away, was coming to fruition as it should, at home, among its own people. I smiled at him. He did not know me but I did know him.

"You must quit India!" He demanded. This time more gently, almost kindly, in the face of my smile. I could have kissed him, despite the breath.

"Have a heart. I've only just arrived." He grinned at me, exposing pink gums and a violently red tongue. I stepped past him and moved on. My journey was only just beginning.

Acknowledgements

My first and greatest thanks must go to my husband, Mike for his open-hearted generosity in letting me plunder his history and ransack his memories. He is the beacon and guy rope of my life.

I also owe huge thanks to our daughter, Ilona Mannan, whose literary gift so far exceeds my own, for her patience, insight and meticulous help with both texts.

I am also grateful to my publisher, Patricia Borlenghi, whose incisive yet sensitive notes have been invaluable.

I also wish to thank:

Nadia Ostacchini, a beautiful and dynamic powerhouse of a girl, who with great charm and purpose, found me my publisher.

Penny Culliford, a gifted writer and wonderful human being, for her friendship, encouragement and profound and unshowy kindness.

Acknowledgements

Edmund Dehn, who listened to my ramblings about a still nascent novel, then lent me his out of print copy of *A Chelsea Concerto* by Frances Faviell, a personal account of living in London during the Second World War. It remains, among the many I have read, for me the most compelling and evocative description of those times and what it must have felt like to live in a city that became a battle zone.

My late uncle, George Rogers, DFC, whose detailed description of an Atlantic convoy, informed me not only of its composition and journey, but also of what it felt like to be on one.

Thanks too to Paul Anthony Barber for his encouragement and support and to Teresa Jennings for her perceptive and unstinting kindness and help.

And then there's Jenny. Jenny Patrick has been the mid-wife of most of my creative endeavours for more years than either of us would care to admit to. First as an actress and then a writer, she has bullied and cajoled, encouraged and inspired me, always with love and laughter, making me feel that the better acted scene, the more expressive phrase was within my grasp, if I would only reach for it. She has egged me on relentlessly and I have been infinitely richer for it.

Bibliography

My main source of material for this book was the treasure trove of Mike's family archive – the letters, diaries, photographs and documents kept by Juanita and Lal.

Of the many excellent books I read on the period in print and on line the most notable were:

A Chelsea Concerto by Frances Faviell. Dean Street Press

London At War by Philip Ziegler. Pimlico

Forgotten Voices of the Second World War by Max Arthur. Ebury Press

We Remember The Blitz by Frank and Joan Shaw. Ebury Press

We Danced All Night: A Social History of Britain Between the Wars by Martin Pugh. Vintage

New Title

Midnight Legacy by Melanie Hughes

Nita's story continues. She and Rikh arrive in Madras. Rikh's squadron is based in Amballa, one of India's oldest military bases and head of operations for the Combined Allied Forces. Rikh takes part in bombing raids on Burma. Bored and miserable, Nita has an affair with a young pilot. She leaves Rikh and goes to Lahore, 'the Paris of the East'. She discovers she is pregnant when the Second World War ends and communal violence is building up all over India. After meeting up again briefly with Lal, an Indian Prince, Nita finally moves to Dehra Dun. Lal's family, however, are bitterly opposed to their union. In an orgy of violence, India at last achieves her independence.

Publication date: 1 November 2017

Paperback edition ISBN: 978-0-9955386-7-2

#0063 - 051118 - C0 - 216/138/15 - PB - 9780995538658